R★WHEAD

Things to Do In Derby When You're Dead

And Other Stories

By

Noel K Hannan

First published in 2021
by Rawhead
an imprint of Ankh Digital

Book design by Noel K Hannan
Cover illustration by Rik Rawling
Interior illustrations by Derek Gray, Steve Kane, Mister Hughes and Jaroslaw Ejsymont

All rights reserved
© Noel K Hannan, 2021

Printed by Amazon

'A Zombie Called Dad' was inspired by the book 'A Dog Called Dad' by Frank B. Edwards and John Bianchi and is respectfully dedicated to the memory of John.

The right of Noel K Hannan to be identified as author of this work has been asserted in accordance with Section 77 of the Copyright, Designs and Patents Act 1988

To PDawg,
with love once again,
someone much, much more than just a muse,
and without whose input this book
would be so much poorer

Foreword

2020AD. Where to start?

It was a year I am sure we would all rather forget. But as life changed – maybe forever – there were so many things which defined the year which were linked to, but not necessarily inextricably dependent upon, the COVID-19 pandemic. Black Lives Matter. The utter absurdity of the Trump administration. The nightly Downing Street updates and the Spitting Image-lite of the Conservative government, impossible to lampoon said *The Guardian's* satire writers (respectfully, I beg to differ), the Proud Boys and the best armed but worst organized revolution in history, Netflix box set gorging and (ahem) 'working from home', Jackie Weaver and parish council Zoom meetings, masked populations. All these things will be gone forever, like tears in the rain. Unless….

This little collection feels like a snapshot of this time. The stories themselves had taken shape some years ago, in particular the titles, and it was always my intent to come full circle back to my first professional gig of zombie stories, almost 30 years ago now. But once the nightly news briefings began and the endless Sky screen saver ads and grim music of advice and guidance and, well, sometimes what felt like propaganda, began in earnest and the lockdowns loomed, it did feel like an opportunity to dust off these stories and see what I could do with them. The results are here, and you can judge for yourself.

Writing this foreword also gives me the opportunity to thank my partner and now creative collaborator Paula White, for huge input into this book which needs calling out in a much more profound way than a simple dedication (although she gets one of those as well). Without Paula, so many elements of this book would simply be missing, and she is responsible for some major improvements over early drafts, and some significant additional sections as well. I will not embarrass her further by calling those out, but you may (or may not) guess where a feminine hand has been guiding me. Paula, I love you, and I love sharing my creative process with you. Long may that continue.

So, here you go, my first zombie stories in almost three decades, what to expect....?

There is, as ever, only one way to find out.

Noel K Hannan

Hereford

Autumn 2021

MINISTRY OF Z

Illustration by Derek Gray

THE VIRAX OUTBREAK
DAY 58

FIRST MEETING OF COBR(A)

CABINET OFFICE BRIEFING ROOM (A)
WHITEHALL

COBR(A) - Cabinet Office Briefing Room (A) – Virax Pandemic Day 58, the day after Lockdown One. Current UK bodycount – 2,745

The Prime Minister ran chubby fingers through his thick blonde hair. Even by his usual unkempt standards he looked as if hadn't slept for three straight days and been roughly buggered by bad tempered Vikings.

"Health Secretary," he said wearily. "What is the LATEST situation report from the NHS?"

The Health Secretary coughed politely into his fist and shuffled some papers in front of him. He had the air of a man who had taken over from the turtles holding up Discworld, so far out of his depth that all the Baywatch lifeguards who had ever been (including the Hoff, Pamela and Erika) could not have saved him. His clock was ticking, the sweepstake had already started on his resignation date, and he was blissfully unaware.

"Overwhelmed in thirty days, Prime Minister. There is no contingency, we sold all the PPE and excess disinfectants to India following COVID-19. If you recall, this was under your instruction – "

"Yes, yes, I understand. PPE will not save us in this PARTICULAR battle. Foreign Secretary, what does the situation look like INTERNATIONALLY?"

The Foreign Secretary turned in his seat and using a remote control switched on a huge screen behind the COBR(A) table. A world map unfolded across the screen, red dots showing Virax outbreaks, multiplying and growing even as they watched. A ticker in the corner of the screen showed infections and deaths mounting with alarming speed. The font grew smaller as the numbers grew bigger.

"As you can see from the visuals, Prime Minister, the situation is deteriorating rapidly, especially in the United States. Attempts to communicate vital information to the populace is hampered by the fact that many Americans think the nightly news broadcast is the new season of a popular zombie TV series. If you recall your specific advice to the previous President back in March with regards to the potential spread of the Virax - "

"Yes, yes, I recall. Hindsight, Foreign Secretary, hindsight. Always WONDERFULLY crystal clear vision. Now, Defence Secretary, what are our OPTIONS with regards to the Armed Forces?"

The Defence Secretary ran his hand across his balding pate, wiping away a sheen of sweat. "Prime Minister, thank you. As ever, Britain's Armed Forces stand ready to participate in MACA[1], MACP[2], MACC[3] and MAGD[4] tasks as directed by this Cabinet. Or to impose martial law, should it come to that – "

The comment resulted in a wave of guffaws around the table. The Prime Minister, once he had controlled his laughter, reached over and patted the Defence Secretary good-naturedly on the arm.

"Defence Secretary, forgive us, but we are not South Americans now, are we? Let us remain calm. Continue, please."

The Defence Secretary ruffled through a rough notepad in order to buy himself some time to collect his thoughts, and cleared his throat noisily.

"Prime Minister, the Armed Forces are experiencing a similar level of infection to the general populace. A significant proportion of the Army and Royal Air Force have turned or are exhibiting early symptoms, although Tourettes is often very difficult to use as an indicator given the prevalence of profanity in the military environment. The Royal Navy, however, given that we have a significant proportion of the Fleet at sea, remain largely unaffected. They may well be a useful reserve to call upon given the present situation and possible courses of action."

The Cabinet were unusually silent at the Defence Secretary's statement. The Prime Minister cocked his head as if to clear unpleasant thoughts from it, seemed suitably refreshed, and leaned forward with purpose on to the table.

"Thank you, Defence Secretary, for that… *sobering assessment.* Home Secretary, over to you, any GOOD news, perhaps?"

"Prime Minister, I am pleased to report that I do." She could barely contain her glee, rocking in her chair like an excited schoolgirl. The Prime Minister leaned forward, rubbing his hands on his thighs, grateful of a glimmer of good news. The Home Secretary was his favourite Secretary, and he had had *many* favourite Secretaries in his time.

---

[1] Military Aid to the Civilian Authorities
[2] Military Aid to the Civilian Powers
[3] Military Aid to the Civilian Community
[4] Military Aid to Other Government Departments

"Prime Minister, our colleagues in the security agencies have been working tirelessly with the Chief Scientific Advisor and his team, along with Department of Health personnel, to identify Patient Zero. The British public deserve to know how this horrendous disease has managed to penetrate our tight borders."

The Prime Minister nodded sagely. His favourite Secretary was all about *tight* borders, *hard* borders, *strict* borders.

"I am pleased to report that we have identified Patient Zero as an illegal immigrant from Haiti."

The Cabinet barely suppressed a cheer! An illegal immigrant, a black chap from Haiti, was actually responsible for the outbreak. This wasn't just a *Daily Mail* headline, it was true, the Home Secretary had said it herself, and she hadn't lied in, oh, absolutely ages!

The Prime Minister could not suppress his joy. "Home Secretary, you always bring the BEST news. The British public will be OVERJOYED. Have you informed all the usual media outlets?"

"Of course, Prime Minister, and you can expect questions about this on subsequent press conferences. We must ensure that the Chews-"

The Cabinet sucked in a collective breath. The Prime Minister closed his eyes and dropped his chin to his chest.

"Home Secretary, we must never, ever, call them that? Do I make myself clear?"

The Home Secretary's dark features masked her furious flushing and she looked hard at the surface of the table, suitably admonished. She raised her eyes and looked directly at her Prime Minister, channelling the look of a puppy caught pissing on a brand new expensive rug.

"I am sorry, Prime Minister, forgive me. Perhaps we can discuss agreed terminology alone following this COBR(A) meeting…?"

The Prime Minister inclined his head in agreement, and accelerated the agenda.

"Defence Secretary – what are our options for attacking, liberating, invading or otherwise randomly FUCKING about with Haiti in order to show those DEVILS we will not stand for this?"

Daily Press Conference #1, Downing Street, from left to right, the Chief Medical Adviser, the Prime Minister, the Health Secretary. The banner beneath each lectern reads HEAD-BRAIN-SPADE with the orange logo of the sponsoring DIY store discrete in the bottom right corner. The press conference has already been running for ten minutes across all broadcast and Internet media outlets.

PRIME MINISTER – "So to reiterate, we are not instructing the people to KILL the zombies, but if you DO need to KILL a zombie, you should do so using the mantra on the banner below, kindly provided by our SPONSORS. I believe you should also make efforts to ensure that your personal armoury is well stocked and that you carry a suitable WEAPON with you at all times. Our sponsors have informed us that supplies are running low, so shop early!"

Awkward air fist-pump and points down at the banner, grinning.

QUESTION FROM THE MONITOR – "Prime Minister, this is Rowena Smith of *The Custodian*. Are you telling us that we should now be killing the Chewmans? That this is permissible under law and ethically and morally sound?"

PRIME MINISTER – "Rowena, good evening, good to see you again, I am glad the libel case has at last been resolved to allow us to talk again, *ha ha*. Excellent question, excellent, as I would always expect from *The Custodian*. To be clear, I am not TELLING the people to KILL zombies, but I am REITERATING a right to self defence and DIRECTING the people to the best methods by which to do so. Our sponsor's website has a large range of domestic and garden equipment which can be used to great effect in self-defence situations. And remember – HEAD-BRAIN-SPADE!"

QUESTION FROM THE MONITOR – "Prime Minister, this is Bill from Battersby, North Yorkshire. I run a small DIY store in the village, and I am currently sold out of all bladed implements, and cannot get a resupply due to county border closures. Am I right in assuming that the DIY chain sponsoring the HEAD-BRAIN-SPADE campaign has bought one of the major shipment and courier companies along with its air fleet, and has sole permission to enter and exit UK airspace in order to restock its stores?"

PRIME MINISTER – "Bill, good evening, excellent question, excellent, a remarkably well-informed question from a DIY store owner from the

North, if I must say. You are right in that our sponsor has been in the, ah, fortunate position of capitalising on its sudden SURGE in demand and has been able form a partnership with a major shipment and courier service to create a WORLD-BEATING supply chain capability which our Government and our COUNTRY are able to utilise to ensure the flow of vital goods remains UNIMPEDED. Thank you, next question….."

COBR(A) - Cabinet Office Briefing Room (A) – Virax Pandemic Day 88. Current UK bodycount – 12,745

The Prime Minister had taken on the air of a man making his exit plans in his head even as his mouth continued to do what passed for its job. His eyes were as dead as a Chewman and he placed his hands flat on the COBR(A) table as if he was about to sign a unilateral surrender agreement with a much less capable enemy. The fresh ghost of the horrifically ill-fated Haitian expedition hung around his shoulders like an invisible, but heavy, black veil.

"Home Secretary," he said, his voice many octaves lower than it had been weeks earlier. She was no longer his favourite Cabinet member, nor even his favourite Secretary. "Tell me about the *Chewman League*."

The Home Secretary had lost none of her faux jolly hockey sticks enthusiasm. She appeared to be the only participant in the COBR(A) meeting with a consistent heartbeat. The global zombie pandemic had not knocked her off her chosen course by a jot. She was in. Her. Element.

"Prime Minister. The *Chewman League* is a left-wing ideologue organisation which appears to have grown organically around the concept that the *Chews* - "

"Home Secretary!"

"Sorry, Prime Minister, the *Chewmans*……the Chewman League believe that the zombies, or Chewmans, are not really dead, or undead, and therefore deserve rights and privileges like the rest of humanity – *bizarre, I know*…..This has resulted in a popular upswell of opinion and support for this concept to the extent that the First League footballers have been 'taking the head' at matches up and down the country this weekend as a gesture of solidarity with the *Zombie Lives Matter* mantra."

"Home Secretary," the Minister for the Cabinet Office interjected, breaking the protocol of the Prime Minister's dominance of this meeting,

15

puffing out his scrotum-like cheeks in mock outrage, "we may be on the edge of declaring the Chewman League a terrorist organisation, and yet millionaire sports stars are participating in acts of support for them. What does 'taking the head' even mean?"

The Home Secretary acquired the remote for the large COBR(A) briefing screen, fiddled with it for an awkward few minutes before she got the right feed up on the screen, then managed to display a short segment from the start of a *Match of the Day* broadcast. Two First League teams, prior to a Saturday 3pm kickoff, assumed static poses on the pitch with their heads cocked to one side and arms rigidly out in front of them in an exaggerated imitation of the pose which a zombie naturally assumed in the latter stages of infection. There was a significant support for this in the crowds, either through applause or mimicking the action themselves. The camera dwelled on popular First League footballer Mark Ashford.

"Home Secretary," the Prime Minister said, "what are the chances of us make this action illegal?"

Daily Press Conference #5, Downing Street, from left to right, the Home Secretary, the Prime Minister, the Defence Secretary. The Home Secretary looks, frankly, fucking furious.

PRIME MINISTER – "The people of the United Kingdom, I bring you grave news tonight which I feel should only come from the lips of the Defence Secretary."

Defence Secretary and the Prime Minister exchange awkward glances, mouthing at each other and making wild gestures with eyes and eyebrows. This had not been planned or agreed. The Defence Secretary reluctantly takes the mantle.

DEFENCE SECRETARY - "Err, thank you, Prime Minister. Evidently, it falls upon me to announce, that for the first time in the history of the United Kingdom, that we are imposing a period of martial law. We have been left with no choice but to do so, given the deterioration of the domestic security situation and in order to further secure border controls. I would like to offer the floor to questions from our audience."

QUESTION FROM THE MONITOR – "Defence Minister, this is Rowena Smith of *The Custodian*. Can I posit that your actions have just rendered the Home Secretary redundant? That by declaring martial law, incredibly for the first time in our history, that you have assumed command of the judiciary, policing and border management? What is the Home Secretary's reaction to that, and in fact why is she even here tonight?"

HOME SECRETARY (*gritted teeth, barely contained fury*) – "If I may, Defence Secretary. Ms Smith, I suggest you take a closer look at your own understanding of martial law, it is - " Her eyes flick momentarily to the notes on the lectern in front of her. " – a temporary imposition of direct military control of normal civil functions or suspension of civil law by a government in response to a temporary emergency. The key word there, Ms Smith, is *government*. I remain the Home Secretary with responsibility for policing and border controls, augmented at this time by the Armed Forces. And a jolly welcome addition they are too!"

The Home Secretary attempts an upbeat end to her retort – it falls as flat as a decapitated Chewman.

QUESTION FROM THE MONITOR (Rowena Smith again) – "Thank you, Home Secretary, but it remains a fact, does it not, that a significant proportion of the Armed Forces, and the county and metropolitan police forces, have already turned, and that the bulk of manpower now available to yourself and the Defence Secretary is comprised of Royal Navy personnel who, at this precise moment in time, sit offshore from strategic ports, simultaneously enforcing the border controls and awaiting disembarkation instructions for duties onshore. I ask the Prime Minister and the Home and Defence Secretaries this – how on Earth do you expect them to fulfil both missions?"

COBR(A) - Cabinet Office Briefing Room (A) – Virax Pandemic Day 120. Current UK bodycount – 25,323

The Prime Minister had run out of fresh suits and the chances of finding a functioning dry cleaners was now down to zero. He had fished in a wardrobe and found a voluminous velveteen dressing grown which one of the old retainers at No 10 assured him had once belonged to Churchill. The Prime Minister thought that this was incredibly apt and ensured the official photographer took some suitably posed snaps, but when he slumped into his chair at the centre of the COBR(A) table for the now-daily meeting, he released a cloud of noxious dust and live moths which hung around him like a cartoon fog for the rest of the session. It was telling that the other Cabinet Ministers present neither commented nor appeared particularly aware of this.

"Chief Medical Adviser," the Prime Minister drawled, struggling to articulate the long title but apparently incapable of abbreviating it, "I understand you have some…chiefly medical advice for us. Please enlighten us."

The Chief Medical Adviser had rarely been directly invited to brief COBR(A) despite his permanent presence in the meetings, and more often than not stood mute witness to the idiocy of government policy being vomited up into the faces of the populace every night at the press conferences. He had been an early opponent of the HEAD-BRAINS-SPADE mantra but had been vetoed by the Chancellor who revealed just how much money the DIY giant had placed on the table. Not to mention how much had gone directly into back pockets.

"Prime Minister, thank you for the airtime." Despite his weariness, the CMA was alert and bright and precise in his speech, in marked contrast to his Ministerial colleagues. He had concise notes in a neat book in front of him, in addition to a PowerPoint presentation of maps, charts and diagrams on the screen behind him, progression controlled by a flunky. The screen currently showed a map of the UK with the largest centres of zombie infection marked dramatically with cartoon skulls, like the planned tour route of a heavy metal band.

"Prime Minister, Cabinet members, you asked me several days ago to produce an assessment of the 'herd immunity' approach which has been suggested by several members of this Cabinet and my colleagues in the scientific community. Here is my response. Next slide please."

    The flunky clicked the PowerPoint forward. The next screen had a single word in large font size in the centre of the screen, black text on white background.

NO

There was a rustling restlessness in the Cabinet. The Prime Minister cast around the room for support and, finding none, shifted in his seat and broke the silence.

"Now, listen here Chief Medical Adviser, we expected something more of a - "

"Perhaps my slide is not clear enough, Prime Minister. It will not work. This is not a novel Coronavirus, something which we can limit with good hygiene, lockdowns and vaccines. It is a plague of Biblical proportions. There are corpses rising from graveyards - "

"Perhaps it is the title, Prime Minister?" the Minister for the Cabinet Office cut in over the CMA. "Herd implies dumb animals, cattle, sheep - "

"Sheep live and travel in flocks, not herds," the Environment Minister interjected, anxious for some airtime. The Minister for the Cabinet Office waved him to silence, his disdain for 'experts' well-documented.

"The people will never accept being part of a herd, Prime Minister," the Minister for the Cabinet Office continued, pointedly directing his statements away from the rest of the room. "Perhaps if we gave it a different name – collective immunity?"

"Or *Community Immunity?*" This from the Special Adviser. Like the CMA, he rarely verbalised at COBR(A) meetings, preferring instead to work his Rasputin-like talents behind the scenes, whispering into the ears of those in power. A ripple of admiration ran around the room, infectious.

"*Community Immunity!*" the Prime Minister exclaimed, a grin breaking his mood. He reached to his right and clasped the Special Adviser around the shoulder in a bear-like grip. "*Community Immunity!* Well done, Special Adviser, well done. Ensure that is minuted and circulated."

The CMA stood up. The room ignored him and continued to congratulate the Special Adviser.

"Next slide please. This is a graphic showing the results of initial testing into various substances which may be of use in inhibiting zombie behaviours. As you can see, there are positive results from the use of minced sheep brains which appears to dampen down the worst of the aggressive zombie traits, rendering them, well, sheep-like in some respects. Efforts to synthesise this are being hampered by lack of access to scientific facilities, dangerous local and national travel conditions for the research scientists, and the collapse of communications infrastructure preventing large datasets from being transmitted."

The Prime Minister appeared interested again in what the CMA had to say. "That is fascinating, Chief Medical Adviser, but we must be careful not to sow false hope at this early stage. Can you send that report to the COBR(A) printer please?"

The flunky carried out the action in response to a nod from the CMA. The COBR(A) laser printer hummed into life, and a sheaf of pages slid smoothly out, straight on to feed tray which dropped them neatly, and noisily, into a networked shredder. The Special Adviser had assured him that this was the cutting edge of information security, and it had worked well for them all so far, as it would in any future enquiry.

The CMA assembled his own papers neatly and pushed them into the centre of the table.

It was over.

Daily Press Conference #13, Downing Street. Lectern #1 is empty, a defeated and downcast Prime Minister occupies Lectern #2, and Lectern #3 is occupied by the Special Adviser in a CHEWMAN LIVES MATTER hoodie.

QUESTION FROM THE MONITOR – "Prime Minister, this is Dave Angel from Skyfall News. What is your reaction tonight to the shocking scenes from Liverpool earlier today as the aircraft carrier HMS Queen Elizabeth attempted to dock?"

The Prime Minister continues to look at the floor, apparently unaware of his surroundings. The Special Adviser allows the awkwardness to continue for a moment longer than necessary, then reaches across the lecterns, passing the Prime Minister a note and nudging him gently. The Prime Minister appears to wake up.

"Ah, Dave, good question, thank you. The Queen Elizabeth, yes, tragic, tragic. Our THOUGHTS go out to those who have lost their lives and to their families at this time. I understand that the situation there has been brought under control.....?" *He looks to the Special Adviser for special advice. The Special Adviser shakes his head sadly.* "Or not. Not under control. But I am CONFIDENT it will be under CONTROL soon."

On the screen to the side, Dave Angel holds up the front page of a newspaper with a graphic photograph of the Queen Elizabeth listing badly in her moorings at one of the Liverpool docks, zombies pouring over her canted decks, sailors and marines jumping for their lives into the cold waters of the Mersey. Dave starts to speak but is cut away to another talking head whose webcam is at a strange malevolent angle, looking right up a posh lady's nose.

QUESTION FROM THE MONITOR – "Prime Minister, I am Dame Judith Jones, head of the independent education watchdog, LEARN[5]. Prime Minister, I understand that in the worst affected areas, what you have designated as Tier One or Zombie Free Fire Zones, your government will be imposing what has been termed 'Learning Lockdowns' on schools whereby teachers and pupils will isolate fully within the school environment, protected by the security forces and allowed to progress with their education in safety. While LEARN supports this move, we do have to ask, how will these children eat, Prime Minister? How will the children eat?"

The Prime Minister has reverted to his catatonic state. The Special Adviser scribbles something hastily on a note and passes it over, this time with a harsher nudge, more akin to a poke.

PRIME MINISTER – "Dame Judith….always a pleasure…..Dame Judith….the kids will eat free…."

The Special Adviser receives a message on his tiny invisible headset, **The taxi is here***. He responds discretely, "*Roger that, we are on our way. No one needs to see this.*" This is picked up by the studio microphones and broadcast even as transmission from the location is abruptly cut. They are the last words broadcast from No 10 for some time to come.*

---

[5] Lifelong Education And Responding to Needs

The screens blank, the cameras abandoned, two stressed-looking soldiers in full body armour and holding their assault rifles at the ready enter the studio.

"Prime Minister, Special Adviser, please come with us." *They are ushered from the studio, through the corridors of No 10, and out into Downing Street, where a Warrior armoured vehicle is awaiting, its back door open and engine idling. In front of it is a Challenger 2 tank, completely battened down, pointing its gun and its mantlet straight out into Whitehall. There are no police officers on the black metal gates protecting Downing Street, but there is a herd of Chewmans, piling up on the ironwork and climbing over each other in an effort to breach the perimeter and get to their feed. The Prime Minister sees one tumble over the top as he his bundled unceremoniously into the back of the Warrior, the Special Adviser tossed on top of him, the armoured door clanging shut and one of the soldiers shouting up to his comrades in the turret,* "We have them, let's go!"

The command is passed from the Warrior to the Challenger, whose engine roars and lurches the armoured beast forward, just thirty metres or so from the gates, which are now spilling Chewmans into Downing Street like an undead waterfall. The Challenger surges on, elevating its gun to avoid a barrel strike on the gate, and crushes Chewmans under its tracks. It breaks through the gates with a terrible screech of rending metal and the screams of Chewmans being torn apart, and then pauses momentarily on the street, as if debating whether to turn right, toward the river, or left, toward the city. There is a brief conflab over the radio and the tank executes a neutral turn to the right, shaking off Chewman boarders and the remnants of the gate, heading toward the river. The Warrior follows suit, its chaingun opening up to the left and right as its turret rotates, carrying the remains of the UK government in its armoured shell, to safety, for now at least.

Special Report, Skyfall News. Special Correspondent Dave Angel.

"Chaotic scenes at Downing Street this afternoon as the Prime Minister is whisked to safety at an unknown location, and is now unavailable for further comments. One of his last acts before becoming incommunicado was to 'promote' the former Health Secretary to the newly created role of Minister for Zs, and hand him sweeping executive powers if not the resources to carry them out. As the new Minister for Zs no doubt struggles with the realities of his new role, the question must be asked, is anyone really left in charge?"

KIDS EAT FREE

Illustration by Steve Kane

The village of Battersby, North Yorkshire. 0900. Day 1, Lockdown 2

"Class – Class - CLASS! Good morning, class, and welcome to day one of our new lockdown schedule. Before we start, I have new message for you from the Minister of Z, please look into the screen...."

The video wall in the classroom was a recent government-sponsored technical enhancement and Ms White, of Battersby Academy, was very pleased with the improvements to her learning environment. There was a High-Definition webcam with a wide-angle lens mounted into the frame, and it allowed both the participation of those schoolchildren who hadn't made it into the compound pre-lockdown, and the possibility of a daily motivational message from a cabinet minister. On Day One, that privilege of course went to the newly appointed Minister of Z.

"Schoolchildren of the United Kingdom, good morning, and welcome to a whole new week of vital, world-beating, appropriately-funded education!"

The chinless wonder that was the Minister for Z, former Minister for Health and Social Care (recently sacked) beamed out at them from their expensive video walls. There was an awkward pause. He had a nervous tic, a spontaneous inappropriate laugh even when he was delivering incredibly bad news, and it was one of the reasons is tenure as Minister for Health and Social Care had been short and traumatic. That, and the fact that his term had coincided with the worst pandemic since, oh, the last one. And then some.

"School and education is, like, really, really important. I remember my school days very fondly. I wasn't a model pupil-" *(awkward conspiratorial wink)* "- and I really wish I could wind back the clock and go back and pay attention and, well, just learn more *stuff*!"

Inane grin and awkward silence as the nation's schoolchildren and teachers looked in, the former with boredom, the latter with mounting horror. Here was a man you wouldn't trust to walk a stranger's dog. Yet he had been handed arguably the most important role in the present crisis. This seemed, however, par for the course for the current administration.

"So, schoolchildren of Britain, I say to you today, if you are isolated at home on Mooz, or confined to your schools and classrooms, listen to your parents, listen to your teachers, and focus on your learning. Your learning is so important. Your learning will enable us to learn our way out of this crisis. Learn, learn, learn our way to freedom!" Awkward fist pump which ends up a bit like a Nazi salute and a bit like a Black Power symbol, which throws up all kind of dichotomies, but probably largely lost on the audience. Fading image of rippling Union flag and a flat version of the National Anthem. No one had been forewarned about this, so no one stood. As awkward moments went, it was as awkward as, well, just about the most awkward thing you could possibly think of. Like your trousers falling down when you're stood on the assembly stage.

A semblance of normality returned to Ms White's classroom. She took the unexpected moment of calm to glance around the room, to the dozen children arrayed behind desks in front of her, appropriately socially distanced, and the huge video wall adjacent to her own desk, where another dozen children, caught at home by the unexpected lockdown or already exhibiting early-stage symptoms, or co-habiting with family members with the same, stared out at her from a mosaic of individual images. Eager faces all. She wondered how many would survive the term, then turned sadly to her own computer, and began the day's lessons.

The unexpected lockdown had been, well, unexpected. Emergency measures by their very nature are generally unplanned and hurriedly enacted, especially if totally unforeseen, and the urgings of the scientific community to lockdown the country in situ immediately had been accepted and imposed with startling speed. You remained where you were – workplace, home, school – wherever life support could be provided in terms of sanitation, habitation, warmth and succour. The timing of the announcement could have been better, but most kids ended up quarantined at school. Ms White found herself in the unenviable position, as an academy schoolteacher specialising in life sciences, delivering lessons on her core subjects, but also mathematics, English and French, as if she had never moved on from the primary school. Needs must, in these extraordinary times.

Day One unfurled broadly as Ms White had expected. Lesson plans were explained, assignments were set. The children, as children do, proved quite flexible to the unusual conditions they were expected to operate within. She tried to engage the children on the Mooz screens as positively as she could those physically in the classroom, and they'd had plenty of experience of that, but she couldn't intervene properly when they chose to mute her or wander off, and several were obviously engrossed in games on other devices out of shot.

"David!"

"Yes, Miss?"

"David, put your cat down, we are in the middle of a lesson."

David, on a Mooz session, looked at the cat he had tightly by the throat, just in shot. He was dribbling.

"Miss….?"

"Yes, David?"

"Errr…FUCKING CUNTY BOLLOCKS FUCK YOU, MISS!"

And David took a big bite out of the cat's neck, as she fumbled with her computer to end his session and alert the authorities to a confirmed infection location. She prayed they would get there before David turned completely and ravaged his entire household. Her email pinged as the security forces' automated system confirmed her call in and thanked her for her model citizenship. The Mooz screen quietly rearranged itself to remove David's presence and in the background the database silently updated itself to mark his unfortunate demise, and drop him from the morning register.

Later, after the end of the school day and the children had had their (initially chaotic) 'quiet time' between lessons and dinner, Ms White came into the makeshift dormitory of camp beds they had arranged at the far end of the school hall, huddled under the assembly stage. Two neat rows of girls and boys in sleeping bags.

"Children," she said. "I have just had a message which promises to be a very special treat for you, very soon. I won't spoil the surprise but…..you should be VERY excited!"

That night, Marlene turned suddenly and killed two other children before Nathan beheaded them all with a handy shovel he had acquired from the caretaker's room. Ms White hadn't even woken, and was faced with the carnage when she roused them for breakfast the next morning. The kids, as ever, took it in their stride. Here, then, was the new normal, for them all.

0900. Day 4, Lockdown 2. "You have no authority here!"

The schooldays settled quickly into a routine and Ms White didn't lose any more pupils in those first few days after the initial lockdown and that traumatic night. She did start to worry about the sudden aggression with which Nathan had ended the situation that night, and he had taken to keeping his prized shovel by his desk during the day, and to hand by his camp bed at night, like a soldier with his rifle. She was in no position to criticise or admonish him, but she did think a quiet personality cult was building around him which could start to challenge her authority. She was going to start reading *The Lord of the Flies* with them today, and then thought better of it. No point giving them a user manual.

She was, however, concerned about the dwindling supplies in the kitchen. There had been little time to stock up when the lockdown was introduced and a school kitchen rarely held more than a week's supply. There was very little fresh fruit and vegetables, almost no meat, and a reasonable supply of canned food of varying types. She would have to be inventive if she was to keep the children well fed before the Army could bring on their first resupply, as she had been promised from Day One, by the Prime Minister himself, that the kids would eat free.

The Mooz sessions were also proving challenging. There was little she could do to prevent those children left at home from getting distracted, leaving the room or otherwise failing to participate fully in the lessons. But she also started to see parents loitering in the background, pulling up chairs and taking notes, and it wasn't long before her email inbox clanged with the following:

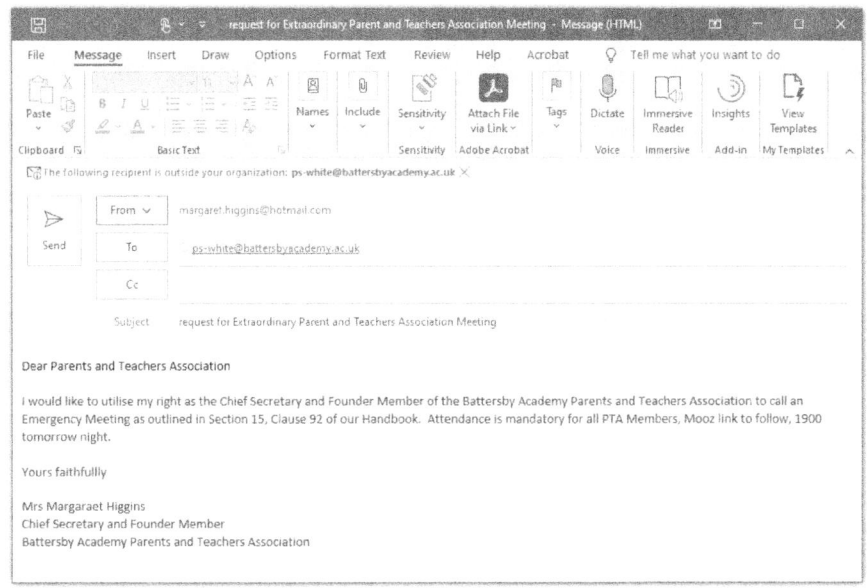

Mrs Higgins…..as if life couldn't get any worse. She was a battered old bag from another era, an elderly woman whose children had left the school decades before and who continued to control the PTA like some Mafia don, surviving a series of head teachers and the odd attempted coup, and who had now reared her blue-rinsed head to make Ms White's life even more miserable. Zombies and Lockdowns she could cope with. Mrs Higgins, she could not.

At 1900 prompt, the Mooz session pinged into life, a grid of eight screens with a couple double-occupied by two adult faces but most just single men or women. Other than the florid harridan occupying the top left of the screen, with everyone else muted, the faces looked uniformly terrified. Mrs Higgins PTA meetings were the stuff of legends. Horrible legends, like the ones with monsters and death and things like that. Exaggeration? Read on….

Mrs Higgins was the controller of the Mooz session and as such had the power to mute, unmute, hand control over (never going to happen) or otherwise end the session for any other participants. Ms White surveyed the faces, recognising some of her teaching colleagues and a

33

few parents she knew, and other parents she didn't. One man, Bob Andrews (Nathan's dad, she noted) had his hand up already and was being pointedly ignored by Mrs Higgins as she started into the meeting proper. He hit the button to make the hand go up and down so it would flash, as if he knew this annoyed Mrs Higgins. It did.

"Good evening everybody. Can I call to order the 95th (Emergency) meeting of the Battersby Academy's Parent and Teacher Association, chaired, as ever-" – flash of a sweet smile like that of a cheetah about to take the hind legs off an antelope – "by myself, Mrs Margaret Higgins, Chief Secretary and Founder Member of the Battersby Academy's Parent and Teacher Association."

Mr Andrews' hand continued to flash. Mrs Higgins continued to ignore it.

"Now, as is the correct protocol for Emergency Meetings, I will take a quick canter through our current financial position. In deference to the Emergency Meeting, I do not propose to formally review the recent accountancy audit, so this should take us no more than forty five minutes. I trust that is acceptable to all members?"

There was rarely any dissent to Mrs Higgins' decision making. Dissent meant that meetings which were formally scheduled for three hours could run to five. Few people had the stamina for that.

Mrs Higgins huffed and appeared to notice for the first time Mr Andrews's flashing hand. She reluctantly acknowledged and unmuted him.

"Mr Andrews, good evening, I saw your hand was up, there was no need to make it flash in such an irritating fashion. Imagine if everyone did that, it would be like an emoji Nuremberg rally. Now, what point of order would you like to make?"

Mr Andrews looked red faced and frustrated already. His camera was at a low angle and his aspect portrait-orientated, as if he was Moozing from a propped up phone. The camera angle was completely unflattering and he had the air of a madman before he had even opened his mouth.

"Mrs Higgins, we are all very busy people. You have called this meting with almost no notice, and indicated it as mandatory. Do you have any idea of the kind of pressures we are living under in these terrible times? I do not have time to waste on financial matters of this PTA-"

"Mr Andrews, I have muted you. You know I have an aversion to acronyms. Please use the full title of the Battersby Academy Parents and Teachers Association in all official matters, including – especially! – this formal if Emergency Meeting. That is all I have to say on the matter."

Unusually, she unmuted him for a second, perhaps by mistake, and he was in full flow, not even having noticed he had been muted, spittle flying from his lips.

"- queuing for water for the rest of the night! I demand to see my son, Mrs Higgins, I would like Ms White to show us the children and show us they are fit and well and being looked after. That is a good use of our time and resources, Mrs Higgins, not your inflexible protocols and bloody PTA-"

Mrs Higgins muted him once more and huffed sadly. He noticed this time and started typing furiously into the chat window

<You have no authority here! No authority at all!!!!!>

Mrs Higgins smiled.

"Oh, but I do, Mr Andrews. I do. Goodbye Mr Andrews, you are now banned for the next formal scheduled meeting." And she kicked him off the Mooz call with no more ceremony. The chat ignited.

<Did she just kick him out?>

<Can she do that???>

<Well, I think he was being disruptive. Well done Mrs Higgins!>

<I don't think we have a protocol for this, the Handbook was last updated in 1995, we didn't have Mooz then>

"Order, order!" Mrs Higgins was becoming agitated by the chat and was furiously shuffling papers in front of her. Ms White had a sudden flash of memory of Mr Andrews at a parents evening, he was a gardener she seemed to think, and that would explain Nathan's prowess with the shovel a few nights ago. She also recalled that the Andrews family lived quite close to Mrs Higgins, perhaps in the same street. She brought up the school's database as Mrs Higgins launched into her – now delayed – forty five minute financial assessment.

Andrews, Nathan
1 Acacia Avenue
Battersby

Higgins, Margaret
5 Acacia Avenue
Battersby

Ms White stared at the screen, horrified. Mr Andrews was two doors away from Mrs Higgins and utterly livid. What did she think he was capable of?

Mrs Higgins looked momentarily distracted. Without muting, she turned and called to her husband, out of shot, "Arthur? What was that? Is someone at the door? Arthur?"

A sudden crash had her reaching for the mute button but as she did so the bedroom door burst in behind her and Mr Andrews, red-faced and wild eyed, stormed into the room with a shovel held high. The shovel was already blood-stained. Mrs Higgins turned and raised her hands ineffectively to her face as Mr Andrews dealt her a savage blow with the shovel, a blow which forced her to the floor and out of shot. He continued to rain blow after blow as gore geysered up into his face and over his forearms.

Eventually, he stopped. He looked into the camera, as if noticing it for the first time. He unmuted the microphone and leant in, his face dripping with blood and brains.

"I declare this session of the....the...fucking P-T-fucking-A!....closed."

0900. Day 6, Lockdown 2. Hunger Games.

Ms White read through the clipboard inventory for the third time, but the story didn't get any better. They were running out food. If they didn't get a resupply soon, the cupboard would be bare within two days. She had already cut their rations twice and the children were getting very, very hungry. She put down the clipboard on the kitchen counter and pinched the bridge of her nose, sighing heavily. This was starting to take its toll on her.

"*Miss....?*"

She turned and was faced with Nathan Andrews, shovel in hand, and a little retinue of boys and girls around him. The shovel was never far from his side, and after seeing the skill with which his father wielded it, she had no wish to risk the same from his son. He had sensed she was scared of him, and he was trying that for size, little acts of defiance or insolence during class, nothing outright rebellious just yet, but small instances of being slow to react to instructions or sly jokes at her expense. She had no idea if he knew anything about what his father had done to Mrs Higgins.

"Yes, Nathan? Can I help?"

"How much food we got, Miss? Doesn't look like much to us. Are we going to go hungry, Miss?"

"Don't worry, Nathan. Everything is going to be alright. Now, take your friends back to class while I finish up here. We have a Physics session starting in a few minutes time."

Nathan paused, leaning on the shovel.

"My dad says that the Prime Minister is a liar, Miss. And that the Army doesn't really exist anymore. He says no one is coming now, Miss, is that right?"

Ms White swallowed hard. "That's not right, Nathan. I am sure your father......means well, but he is wrong. The Prime Minister was telling the truth when he said the kids would eat free, and Mark Ashford has been touring schools doing just that. In fact-"

Nathan hefted the shovel to his shoulder in a sudden movement which alarmed her and made her jump.

"I hope so, Miss, I really do. You wouldn't like me when I'm hungry."

And he took his little retinue off into class, because he wanted to, and not because she told him to. Ms White breathed a sigh of relief and whispered a quiet prayer for imminent salvation.

0900. Day 8, Lockdown 2. A Very Special Visitor.

"Boys and girls, I would like to make a big welcome for a very special visitor today. He has come a long way to see you. Please say hello to……..Mark Ashford!"

Flanked by two huge soldiers in full HAZMAT and body armour, the footballer cut a diminutive figure in what looked like a posh fitted designer space suit. In his hands were two large shopping bags filled with food. Baguettes jutted awkwardly in case someone didn't realise what was inside. He placed the bags down in front of him and took a step back, apparently reluctant to fully enter the classroom. The soldiers' faces were not visible however their body language, as much as that could be interpreted behind layers of protection, betrayed their nervousness. No one wanted to be here, that much was evident.

"Hello, children," Mark said weakly, muffled by the helmet. "I promised that the schoolchildren of Britain, forced to isolate in their schools and homes, would not go hungry, and I am here today to make sure I make good on that promise." He indicated the two bags of shopping in front of him. The children stared back impassively.

Ms White coughed politely into her fist. "Err, children, where are our manners? Can we please thank Mark for coming to see us and bringing us all this lovely food? Perhaps a little round of applause?"

She began to clap and for a few awkward seconds she was the only one doing so, then a couple of the children joined in, but the overall effect was one of acute embarrassment. Then Johnny slipped from his chair and was the first to rummage in the bags, ignoring the footballer and the soldiers, followed by Charlotte and then Nathan and then Charlie, all pulling items from the bags and tossing aside what they didn't like. Ms White, appalled at their behaviour, stepped forward to intervene.

Charlie raised his head from the bag. There was blood dripping from his chin and a handful of raw steak in his fist.

"Miss," Charlie said. "My Dad says Mark Ashford is A FUCKIN' WANKER!"

Ms White recoiled in horror. The two soldiers brought their assault rifles to bear but were jostled by Mark Ashford as he panicked and tripped over them in his effort to escape, bringing them all crashing to the floor. The soldiers were too heavily laden to get to their feet quickly and before they could, there was a child on each of them, tearing off the protective equipment with a speed and strength way beyond their size and age, and then they were joined by other children, as the Virax ripped through the class like wildfire.

"FUCKING FOOTBALLERS!! MY DAD SAYS SHOOT THE LOT OF THEM!"

Mark Ashford found himself trapped under one of the soldier's armoured legs. He wriggled and shunted to get out, but before he could one of the children was on him, snarling, and his helmet had been smashed. He saw the soldiers' weapons getting torn from their grasp and hurled aside, even as one manage to let off a desultory burst of fire into the classroom ceiling. A tidal wave of children overwhelmed him, and he was gone.

Ms White, terrified, had retreated to her desk and packed herself into the tiny space between the drawers. She huddled there, sobbing, curling herself into a tight ball, trying not to make any noise and attract attention but knowing she was doomed. The sounds of carnage from the classroom were horrific. She heard the soldiers screaming, bone crunching, slobber and slurping and ripping. She buried her head into her knees and waited for the end.

After a while, it went quiet. She heard a door bang at the end of the corridor and the sound of running. She lifted her head and looked out from under the desk. Charlie was crouched there, his face and hands bright red with blood. He was on all fours and was sniffing at her, his eyes yellow and wild. She shut her eyes tight and held her breath. He moved a little closer, to within a hands' distance, and inhaled deeply. His eyes held no recognition, but something was stopping him from attacking her. Was there some shred of Charlie left in there that would not let the beast he had become kill his favourite teacher? She would never know.

There was shouting and screaming from outside. The children had evidently breached the school gates and were out into the street. Charlie lifted his head, snorted and ran with his pack. Ms White collapsed back into her hidey hole and fumbled for her mobile phone.

"Hello, hello, yes is that Contagion Control? I would like to report an infection incident. Yes, that's right, Fanny White, Battersby

Academy. We need some help. Please send help. Please send....*everyone*."

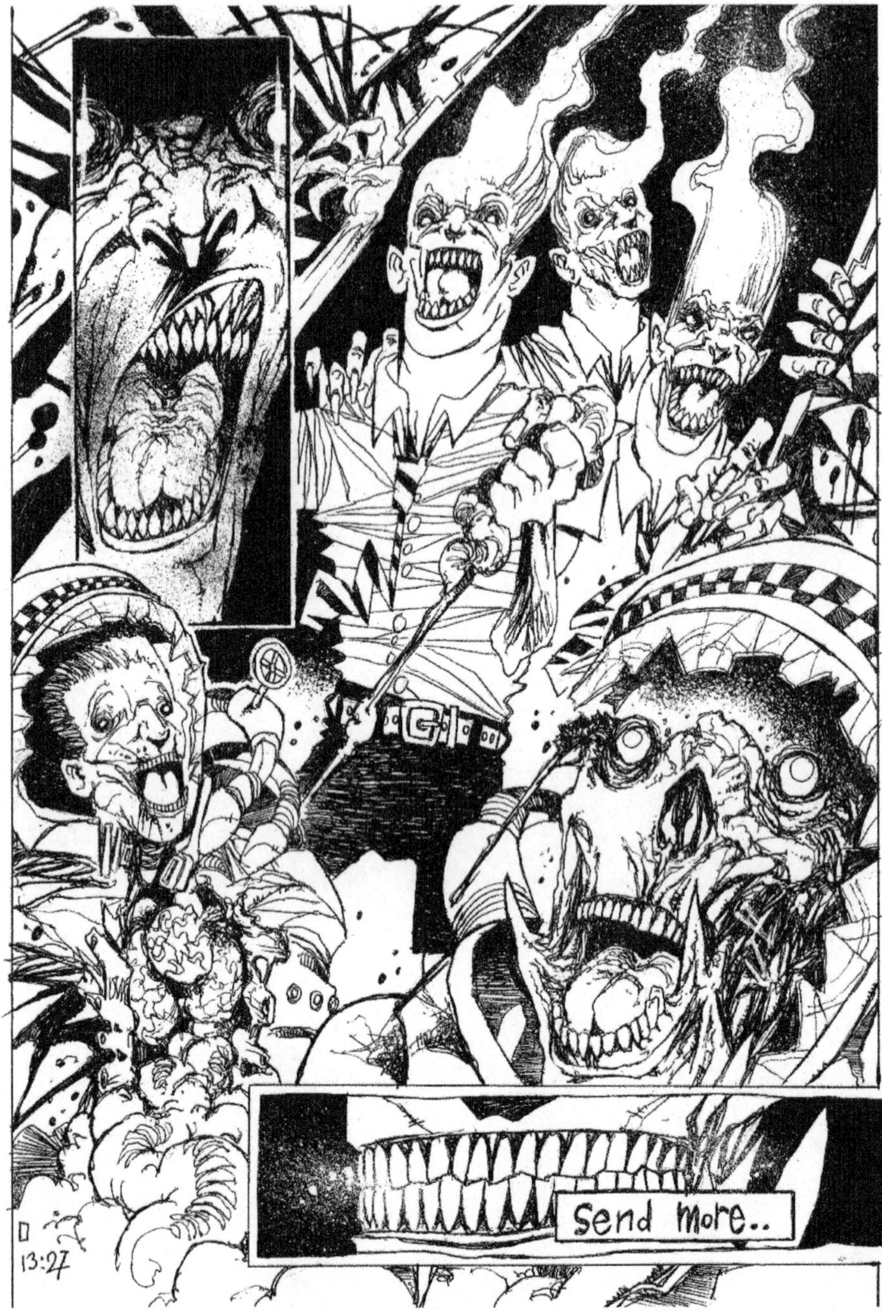
send more..
13:27

THINGS TO DO IN DERBY WHEN YOU'RE DEAD

Illustration by Mister Hughes

Aunt Fanny was going to be so, so worried. They hadn't been home for five days, and they had promised her they would be back within three. Julian had held Fanny tightly and squeezed, and she had made him swear Honest Injun that he would phone her if they were delayed, and he did swear, even though he knew that the final cellular network had collapsed and the Chewmans had overrun the Last Call Centre, which meant their phones were now no more than pocket warmers connected to *Fuckall Anywhere* $^{(TM)}$ for the foreseeable future. Julian sighed at the thought and leaned into his canoe paddle, cutting hard into the cold waters of the Derwent.

"Dick?"

"What, Georgina?"

"*George*, you mean. Dick......?"

"Yes, *George*?"

"*Dick*....why do you always have to be such a *cock*?"

"Ha fucking ha, *Georgina*. Julian, bring us alongside. Timmy needs a shit."

Julian brought them alongside. He beached them gently at a shale curve before the A601 bridge, just to the north of the Bass Recreation Ground. Timmy hopped off the boat and curled out an impressive steaming dog log on to the wet aggregate, looking over his shoulder with smug canine satisfaction. Julian dug his oar into the shore and jumped out, ruffling the little cocker spaniel behind the ears, glad he had not shit on the boat, again. Anne followed on Timmy's trail, as she always did.

Julian moved to the front of the deep Canadian canoe, seized the grab handle and hauled the boat a few feet on to the shale, enough to stop it from drifting off into the river but not enough to keep everyone's feet dry. Dick was a cock but Julian.....well, Julian was the opposite. And by that, I don't mean a good guy. He was a -

"Can't you pull us a bit further in, Jules? I hate getting my feet wet. I have the most terrible chilblains!"

Dick.... Dick..... if ever anyone lived up to their name, it was Dick. Julian shot him a look which could have silenced a knackered student fridge, if anyone could remember what one of those was, other than an overengineered white cupboard with no ability to keep food fresh, and Dick took the hint. Often cheeky, he would defer to his older brother whenever required. Julian was in charge, and that was that.

Having landed the canoe, Julian headed in the direction Timmy and Anne had taken, under the bridge and toward the scruffy parkland to the west. Ahead lay a typical urban sprawl, vaguely American-style strip malls grouped into loose functions, a couple of budget hotels serving the courts complex and the council offices, a symbiotic outer ring of coffee shops, sandwich companies and 'pubs', all now derelict and no doubt infested with Chewman nests. The fucking Chewies......Julian hated them with a passion. A good day for him was decapitating a hundred Chewmans, their useless corpses writhing in the dirt, and on those occasions, he didn't think it too many.

"FIVE! Heads up! Watch out for the nests! Check your fives and twenties!"

Julian had been in the Army Cadets before the Virax and had learned all the patter from some fat old instructor who had claimed to have served in Iraq and Afghanistan. No one had really believed him, but he seemed to know the language and they had all learned it without really knowing what it meant. Julian shouted stuff like that and other nonsensical phrases like "WATCH YOUR SIX!" and "BACK IN!" and it seemed to do the trick with the others, the rest of the Five, because they were still alive. *For now.*

*Julian......Julian......*he recalled, not for the first time, when he had killed his first Chewman. The Virax pandemic had been at its height and he had been riveted to the nightly news as everyone else had, as the graphs mounted and the experts exported, as experts do, and the politicians prevaricated, as politicians do. He was in one of his first board meetings, invited as a tech grad on behalf of Skyfall Satellite Broadcasting, to see how the 'big boys' played, when one of the board members turned mid-meeting, exhibiting the early symptoms of palsy, twitching, foaming at the mouth, eyes rolling back, a selection of classic Tourettes and snatching at anything edible in the vicinity, before quickly moving on to the medium symptoms of meat and blood lust, animal phobia, hysteria and unresponsiveness, and the later symptoms of total carnage zombie mania, for want of a better term, all in the space of what should have been a routine Agile project management meeting.

The thermal coffee pots had yet to cool when Julian had been forced to leap on the table and stab the executive in the eye with a free biro, penetrating his brain just as the nightly BBC News had instructed (admittedly free biros were not the recommended weapon of choice), and saving the day. Tech grads in Skyfall Satellite Broadcasting rarely had the chance to exhibit such raw courage, but Julian's opportunity to dine out on it was extremely limited, given the subsequent apocalyptic onslaught of the Chews and the apparent total collapse of what had previously passed for civilisation.

"Julian! Over here! You have to see this!"

Julian was shaken from his recollections by Dick's ejaculation. Dick could on occasion be a right pain in the arse, but he was his younger brother, and Fanny would be extremely irritated if he let him come to harm. An irritated Fanny was something none of them really wanted to see.

Dick had positioned himself on a grassy incline overlooking the edges of an abandoned business park. He was hunkered down below the ridge just as their fat Army Cadet instructor had taught them, and was holding a pair of small rubber armoured binoculars. He was looking at Julian. He was pale and hyper-ventilating. Julian slammed down next to him, channelling his inner *Saving Private Ryan* moment, and snatched the binoculars from his brother. He edged up to the ridge and pressed them to his eyes.

"Good……Lord……" Julian softly cursed.

It was getting dark. September twilights crept in early, and the Chewies didn't like the daylight too much it seemed, so their peak activity was after dusk. The hours between late afternoon and early evening seemed to shake and poke the nests, and rouse them from their stupor, putting the smell of meat back into their mushed brains.

And here they were, Derby's entry for Best Mob Ever, filling a business centre car park with Chewies piled high, climbing over each other in a chaotic and frantic effort to get into what looked like an abandoned DIY warehouse, until Julian saw through the binoculars a rough perimeter fence that had been fashioned from multiple layers of chicken wire and Waney Lap fencing (poorly footed, he noted sadly) and what looked like actual humans with shotguns and a few military assault rifles popping heads and just about keeping the Chewies at bay. Julian flicked the binoculars up and his attention was caught by a flickering neon sign mounted high where the original DIY store sign would have been.

The Margaret Thatcher Memorial Miner's Welfare Non-Working Men's Club

Bzzt! The sign buzzed and flickered in the twilight. *Bzzt!*

"Right, take a knee, here's the plan……"

Julian and Dick had returned to the shale beach. Anne and Timmy had returned also, Timmy's chops red and wet with God knows what, and they joined Georgina and the others as Julian sketched out his plan in the damp earth with a snapped car aerial. Timmy stared hard at the dirt plan with the intensity with which he normally considered a simple card trick.

"Situation – probably totally fucked as usual. Disposition of enemy forces – 360 degrees as usual. Atts and Detts – fuck all. Options – limited. Any questions?"

The Four looked back at him, mimicking Timmy's face when considering the card trick. Admittedly, that was far from the best set of orders he had ever delivered.

"Julian," said Georgina, choosing her words carefully, "what *exactly* do you want us to do?"

It is easier to describe what they did rather than Julian's quasi-Army Cadet attempts at an orders session. Julian deduced that there were uninfected humans inside what appeared to be a DIY store repurposed as a 'night club' (there was some debate about the validity of that term) and that they should link up with them. It was a reasonable punt, but they hadn't seen any uninfected humans other than Aunt Fanny for months. It was a gamble, but Julian was the oldest and the smartest and he was in charge. So that was ok.

The mass of Chewmans between their landing spot and the Club was impenetrable. A frontal assault, cutting through with the assortment of martial arts weaponry and DIY tools they had amassed, was suicidal. Julian had noticed a narrow path which hugged the river and led around the back to what would have been the store's garden centre, hung with shredded green netting, where the Chewies hadn't yet herded. He reckoned this was their best bet, and it turned out he was right.

The best route in was back on the river. Chewies, they thought, generally didn't swim. Or at least, not very well. They retrieved their canoe and pushed a little further north and west, Julian up the front of the boat with his samurai sword held out in front of him like he was George fucking Washington (with a samurai sword) and Georgina at the stern, with Timmy sticking his head out like a meerkat. Dick and Anne maintained watching positions inside the canoe.

They dropped quickly through the shallow weir where the water ran fast and they lifted paddles out of the water to allow them passage. There was a wooded island directly in front of them where the current wanted to take them to the north, and under Julian's direction they steered themselves to the south, beaching again at a point on the river where the Chewies had thinned to a vague spread of individuals whom Anne and Dick decapitated with almost absent minded attention while Julian dragged the boat up the shallows again.

The Margaret Thatcher Memorial Miner's Welfare Non-Working Men's Club loomed over them, its neon flickering in the gathering gloom and the tattered flags of *Derby County Nil* cracking and fluttering in the wind, like the battle standards of lost Roman Legions who had wandered too far north in Britannia. If you could call Derby the North – *many did not.*

"Dick. Up my ass. *Now.*"

Dick was up Julian's ass in an instant. So was Georgina. They looked in eagerly for guidance, gripping (respectively) a brush hook (which looked like it was designed for divesting Chewmans of their heads and limbs rather than a tree of its branches) and a double Samurai short sword combination in Tanto configuration, which Georgina had insisted upon because she had been the primary consumer of zombie media before the Virax and as such was their main source of information on such matters, which was a bit like being an expert on science fiction prior to World War 2. But there was a deficit of subject matter experts at this particular moment in time, so Georgina was as good as they had.

"Guys….*and George*……we're gonna leave Anne and Timmy with the boat while we skirmish up to the fence line and make contact with the humans within. I am assuming they will have some kind of entry point we can access and we will take it from there. Once we get a handshake from them, you two will go forward and I will go back for Anne, Timmy and the boat. Got that?"

Georgina frowned. "What does *skirmish* mean?"

Julian rolled his eyes. "*Doh*, George, like, what the fuck? *Skirmish - an episode of irregular or unpremeditated fighting, especially between small or outlying parts of armies or fleets.*"

Georgina rolled her own eyes. "Julian, you fucking dick-"

"What?" said Dick.

"-not you! Julian, shall we just approach the fucking fence or what?"

They approached the fucking fence. They could see figures moving on the other side, wary of their approach but also apparently understanding that they weren't Chewmans and also didn't have long barrelled weapons, so were willing to allow them to approach the portion of fencing not besieged by Chews.

"*Stop right fucking there! Who the fuck are you?*"

Julian held his right fist up. Dick and Georgina halted.

"We are....*the Five*. We are human. Who are you?"

The humans behind the fence held a quick debate. Their spokesperson, a lanky teenager in a hoody, returned to his role as communicator and cleared his throat into his fist.

"I think that we, as the tenants of this safe haven, are the ones who ask the questions. You are.....*the Five*? Where the fuck are the other two?"

Julian rolled his eyes again. "Two are with the boat. One is a girl. One is a dog. Can we come in now?"

There was another quick debate, this time more animated. Julian wondered how they could tell if anyone was turning with the amount of swearing going on.

"You have.....*a girl*?"

Julian's eyes narrowed. He sensed an in. He winked and nodded at Georgina who returned a look which could have burned toast.

"Yes.....*two* to be exact. Is that a......*problem*?"

The spokesperson did not bother to confer. "No! Approach the fence, we are letting you in!"

Julian discretely keyed his walkie-talkie mike on the shoulder of his rucksack. *"Anne, I am coming back for you, bring Timmy and the boat, we're in."*

"Roger, Julian, we are on our way!"

The safe haven had constructed a complex gate system from abandoned and upended vehicles lashed together with chains and ropes, which could be windlassed aside for access or egress. The humans within opened the gate just wide enough for Dick and Georgina to enter, then closed it again and waited until Julian reappeared dragging the boat with Anne, and Timmy jogging alongside. A sudden surge of Chewies off to their flank made Julian drop the boat and wade in with his samurai sword and lop the heads from a few, before picking up the boat and making a dash for the opening gap. It was a good demonstration for the denizens of this safe haven that the Five meant business.

The gate thudded shut behind them. Julian dropped the boat again and stood panting, his hands on his hips, looking around the compound. It was almost dark and the light from the neon sign was practically the only source of illumination, as the mainly nocturnal Chewies were attracted to light sources. The compound had been constructed around a former DIY store but now appeared to be a massive night club. Julian was pondering the logic of this when a thick-set red-faced middle-aged bald man elbowed his way through the young humans clustering around the newcomers and popped out in front of them. He immediately launched into what could only be described as a novel sales pitch.

"Alright, Derby, Derby, Derby!

"Come on in, pussy lovers. Yeah, you heard me right! Here at the Rammed Inn AKA the Margaret Thatcher Memorial Miner's Welfare Non-Working Men's Club, we are slashing pussy in half!

"We got a vast selection of finest Derby pussy, it's a pussy blow out!

"Alright, we got sheep shagger pussy, Marmite $^{(TM)}$ pussy, BAKEWELL TART PUSSY!! Pork scratching pussy, real ale pussy, BLACK! PUDDING ! PUSSY!!

"We got sausage roll pussy, smoky bacon pussy, SCAMPI FRIES PUSSY!!! McDonalds $^{(TM)}$ breakfast pussy, chip shop curry sauce pussy. We even got Finger of Fudge $^{(TM)}$ pussy, barm cake pussy, Nottingham pussy (the best!) and on special - just for tonight - LADY CHATTERLEY'S PUSSY!

"You find cheaper pussy elsewhere? Please report it to Derby City Council via our website and an inspector will be around within a short period to take a formal statement from you.

"I am just kidding of course! You find cheaper pussy elsewhere? FUCK IT!!!!!!!"

The Five stood in a loose semi-circle around the man. He grinned inanely at them, then grabbed Georgina's hand and dragged her good naturedly in his wake toward the club. The Five – or more accurately, the Four - looked in to Julian for guidance. For once, he was lost for words. He shrugged and followed in the man's wake.

The proprietor of the club, and its vociferous spokesman, was Mad Brian. He was a Yorkshireman and wasted no time in ensuring the Five knew that. He had been marooned in Derby at the start of the Virax, unable to return home when the counties had started unilateral attempts to secure their borders, and decided to open a…..nightclub. There was no logic to this, but if it's logic you need, *you may be reading the wrong book. There is no shame in exiting now.*

"You've arrived at a good time," Mad Brian confided to Georgina as he pulled her through the outer foyer into the cavernous club. Music pulsed, basslines thrummed through the walls and doors, and they could see flashing lights and lasers flickering within. Mad Brian seemed unaware that Georgina was actually a girl, which would normally have pleased her, but on this occasion, actually irritated her. He nudged the doors open and they were overwhelmed by noise, heat, smoke, light, sweat and the unmistakeable smell of rotting flesh. A barely dressed female Chewman stumbled past, a tattered sash hanging from her shoulder. Dick raised his weapon to strike and Mad Brian called out,

"STOP! DON'T KILL HER! IT'S A HEN PARTY, AND SHE'S THE BRIDE!"

A hen party…..it was true. The pink sash read *TEAM BRIDE*. They moved gingerly into the club, drawing together as a unit as they always did at times of crisis, shoulder to shoulder, Timmy pawing forward, sniffing the air and growling softly. So many smells, so many Chewmans……! Why were they not attacking? Why were they….dancing? They had never seen anything like this before.

Mad Brian turned and stopped them. He waved his arms in a conciliatory gesture.

"Calm down, calm down. Put your weapons down. We will have no trouble here. We have them all under control, and we use them for our entertainment. Look at me, I am not being the perfect host, let me get you all a drink! Follow me!"

They looked into Julian for guidance once again. Once again he shrugged and dropped his weapon to his side, and followed Mad Brian through the mixed crowds of humans and Chewies. He saw mixed couples embracing, human kissing Chewie, and his stomach flipped. How was this even possible?

Mad Brian corralled them at the bar and ordered a round of beers without asking them what they wanted. It gave them a chance to take in their surroundings, this vast repurposed space with some of its original trappings in place, towering shelves that once held power tools and screws and bathroom cabinets now lit by laser and neon and holding cage dancers, both humans and Chewies, with platform dance floors and DJs in glass pods. The music took a sudden turn to dark gothic rock and *Drink With The Living Dead* by *Ghoultown* boomed out.

Mad Brian randomly distributed frosty bottles of lager and bitter and rather thoughtfully a steel bowl of water for Timmy. There was no opportunity to swap drinks or complain over the din of the music or the press of the crowd, only Mad Brian's voice appeared to have enough volume to be heard.

"Let me explain," he started lucidly. It sort of went downhill from there.

Ergo:

Executive summary – *some daft refugee scientists from Birmingham had found sanctuary in Derby and brought a bit of laboratory kit with them. With said laboratory kit, they analysed Chewie brain matter and figured out that their lust for human brains could be satiated by sheep brains, which made the Chewies docile and even reverted, at least temporarily, some of the worst aspects of Chewie behaviour. One thing led to another, and Mad Brian opened a nightclub which was essentially a Demilitarised Zone between Chewie and human. As long as the supply of sheep brains didn't run out. Any questions? No? Then let us continue....*

While the Five processed this information, the club DJs made way for the house band, who mounted a massive stage made from pallets, lumber, toilets and kitchen units and decimated every human eardrum on the stage with the opening thrum of bass and drums from what would no doubt be a ballad – not.

"Hello Derby! We are Nerdy Cowgirl! Are you ready to rock?"

The crowd assured Nerdy Cowgirl that they were, indeed, ready to rock, and the mixed band of male, female, human and Chewie launched into an apocalyptic opening number entitled *YOU ARE DEAD TO ME, AND I LOVE YOU FOR THAT,* the Chewie drummer maintaining a solid rhythm with radius and ulna devoid of flesh or hands, and no need for drumsticks.

"My love, my corpse, my breath, your stench, you decompose for me, I compose for you."

The human singer was a slight teenage girl swirled in blue tattoos and the darkest eye makeup, swathed in black rags whipped around by stage fans, making her look like a wraith ascended from Hell. She must have been thirty metres from the Five but Julian felt she was looking straight at him, dark eyes boring into his soul.

"You're so dead, you probably think this song is about you, don't you?"

Georgina felt it too. She felt a warm feeling spread through her tummy as she watched the gothy girl work the audience into a frenzy. She saw random body parts lazily arcing on to the stage.

"You're dead to me, but you make me feel alive."

Anne had no idea what was going on, and the beer Mad Brian had thrust upon her had gone straight to her head. She dropped to her knees and hugged Timmy to her. The fur on his back had raised and his ears were tilted forward.

"You're dead to me, let us feast upon the Five."

Dick shot Julian a glance. For the first time, Dick saw fear and confusion in Julian's eyes, and it scared him. Had they both heard the singer right? It was impossible to communicate properly in this environment, but an unspoken message passed between them – *We must be careful.* No shit, Sherlock.

Nerdy Cowgirl wound up their opening number in a crash of boney drums, mashing guitars and wailing vocals, bringing to mind a motorway car crash featuring numerous emergency vehicles and an air ambulance falling from the sky. The singer motioned the audience to a semblance of silence.

"Derby, Derby, we will be back later with the rest of our uplifting set, but until then, let me introduce the headline act this evening, the one you have been waiting for, the one, the only, THE FULL MORTE!"

The club was plunged into darkness. Anne felt herself being groped and was glad that Timmy was by her side, less disadvantaged by the darkness and able to snap and growl at her assailants, human and Chewie, who retreated licking their wounds. Georgina faced no such onslaught, the denizens of the club seemingly unaware, or disinterested, in her gender. She was actually pretty miffed about this.

Julian and Dick went back to back, weapons drawn, Dick hard up against Julian. They assumed their *zanshin* positions, total combat awareness, and waited for the inevitable attack.

On the stage, thin bobbing semi-circles of neon emerged – red, blue, green, yellow, purple, orange – moving across the stage and assembling in a juggling line. Light emerged again with a blast of fire and fireworks and five Chewmen with neon collars were briefly illuminated, ragged flesh draped in the vague semblance of a farmer, a miner, a police community support officer, a cyclist, a soldier and a Woad-daubed barbarian. Lasers strobed and dazzled as they struck poses and the music thudded.

"Flesh! Ah-ha! They'll turn every one of us!" Nerdy Cowgirl, now side stage, provided the thumping soundtrack.

Julian turned to Dick and mouthed *Oh, for fuck's sake!*

The Full Morte filled the stage, working the crowd into a frenzy, tossing items of clothing and accessories into the air as they bumped and ground to the music. Helmets, waistcoats, boots and hats took to the air, snatched greedily by the crowd. A wet body part flopped on to the stage, thrown lazily by a reveller. The 'police officer' picked it up, kissed it lovingly, and tossed it back into the audience. The crowd went wild.

"NASH! Ah-ha!"

"They'll hunt every one of us."

"They'll turn every one of us."

"They'll group like a zombie herd, every man, every woman every child in a mighty NASH!"

Julian gripped Dick and pulled him close. He roared in his ear, *"We will have one chance to get out of here, grab the girls, come with me if you want to live!"*

The Full Morte's act was reaching its crescendo. The Chewie strippers were naked now, and had started to hurl strips of flesh into the crowd. Chewie revellers fell hungrily upon the offerings, and it seemed to be the drug of choice for the humans too. The strippers arranged themselves into a rough line at the front of the stage, hands placed demurely covering their groins, then without further ceremony, ripped off their rotting cocks and hurled them into the crowd, where Team Bride suffered multiple casualties in the fight to catch them like putrid, phallic wedding bouquets.

It was a signal.

A very clear signal.

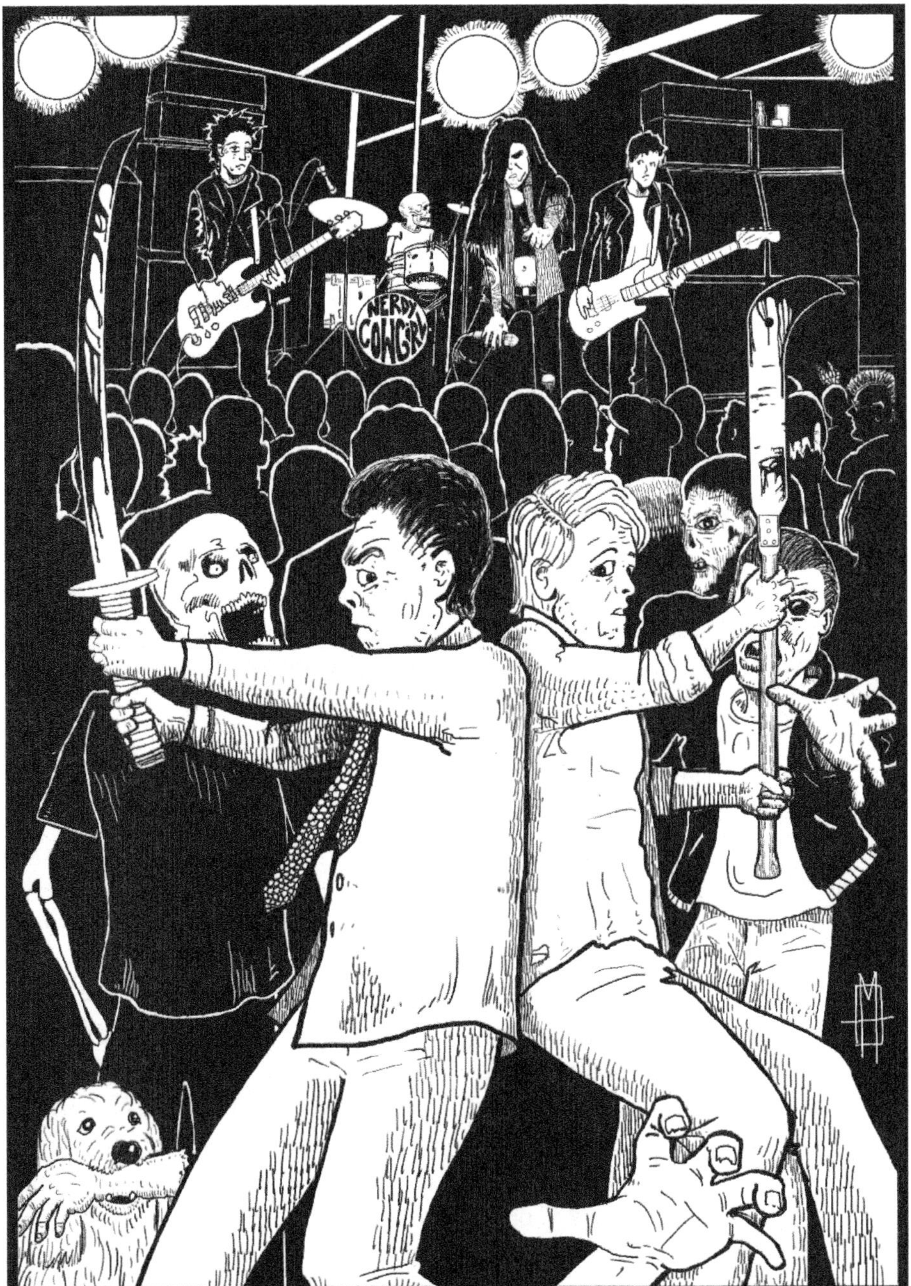
NERDY
COWGIRL

Julian and Dick operated as a very tight unit when the stakes were raised. As human and Chewie alike descended upon them in a frenzy initiated by the Full Morte's *phallus apocalypse* and Nerdy Cowgirl's aural urgings, they created space around them by neatly decapitating any nearby moving target. Georgina, Anne and Timmy had long learned to stay low and let them do their thing unhindered. Georgina had dropped to her knees and was hugging Anne and the dog close, even as Timmy growled and struggled to get free in order to assist in protecting them. He was nothing if not optimistic for a cocker spaniel, a breed who had no formal recorded deaths attributed to them in living history. *Bless.*

As the crowd pulled back momentarily under Julian and Dick's spirited defence, Julian abruptly realised he had killed his first human, as a decapitated corpse thrashed at their feet and jetted blood all over them. But this place……there were no distinctions between human and Chewie, everyone was their enemy, and a bloodlust had risen in the crowd which transcended the distinction. Julian saw Mad Brian, a stricken look on his face, making his way along the bar gripping a cricket bat like a lightsabre, apparently as endangered as the Five were.

"Brian!" Julian hailed. "What the fuck is going on?"

Brian halted and searched for the source of the voice. Julian wasn't totally sure Brian knew who he was talking to, but he called out into the chaos of the club.

"We ran out of sheep brains. Ran out, imagine that, in fucking Derby! Anyway, it was good while it lasted! Have a good –"

And his last words were drowned by a tsunami of Chewmans driving over him, casting aside his pathetic cricket bat like a matchstick. He vanished under the onslaught in a spray of gore.

Both Dick and Julian knew that they could not hold their position. Their only option for survival was to get out of this place, out beyond the perimeter and into open country, where the shambling Chewies could not pursue them at speed. They had not experienced the phenomenon of humans gorged on Chewman flesh, and the swiftness by which the Virax turned them was shocking. Julian turned to Dick, weapon raised, lips pursed to shout a warning when something slammed into his face at high speed and a red mist crossed his vision, taking consciousness with it.

He was back at the conference table. He was naked, of course, such a common self-conscious dream of the confident. He covered his nakedness with his hands while casting his eyes furtively around the room, looking for signs of turning, but in this dream, there were Chewman sentries (or bouncers) on the doors of the opulent chamber (an upgrade on the windowless room of reality) and as such he was confused, but isn't that the natural state of dreams? The anonymous project manager across the table began to spit and foam and

"ARSE!"

Julian awoke and was instantly aware of Georgina's *kukhri* pressed hard to his throat. Her eyes were wide and flared with fear, anger and loathing.
"*What did you say?*" she hissed.
He felt the cold steel press against the vulnerability of his jugular and suppressed the urge to swallow.
"*Ass?*"
Georgina's eyes narrowed. She released the pressure from the blade and backed away, only to be replaced by Timmy, his long snout pressing into Julian's face, sniffing hard, giving a cursory lick, then a confirmatory *woof!* and backing off in search of more interesting fare.
Julian rose on his elbows. He was in what looked like a barn by the rough walls, concrete floor and straw strewn around. It smelled of animals.
"*Georgina.....*"
"*George, for fuck's sake.....*"
"*George...what the fuck happened...where is everyone?*"
Georgina knelt by him and brushed his sweaty hair aside in an absent minded tender gesture.
"*Julian.....they're gone. They are all gone. Dick, Anne – we lost them in Derby in that fucking 'club' or whatever the fuck it was. I just about got you out. There was a pickup truck outside and I got you and Timmy in and here we are.*"
Julian flipped himself over on to his knees, the hard floor unforgiving, and pushed himself to his feet. He felt faint, staggered for a moment against the wall and Georgina's arm, and stepped from the barn.
Hill village, overlooking a city, he thought maybe Derby but it wasn't his patch so hard to tell from up here. The barn was the focus of

a farmyard, and a large farmhouse spread across the face of a hill, no more humans visible. He took a deep breath.

"George-"

"Stop. You've been in a coma or something like that for three days. Anything which comes out of your mouth now is likely to be more shit than you normally spout. So for once, shut the fuck up. Ok?"

That was about as much sense as it needed. He nodded weakly and allowed Georgina to take his left elbow and support him as he stood up.

"We lost them in that fucking 'club', Julian. Why did we even go in there? It was fucking mental. What were you thinking?"

"Pussy?" Julian offered weakly, leaning into Georgina's arm. She pulled him close and gestured up the track.

"Yeah, right, Julian, pussy. Like that ever works out for anyone. You ok?"

Border collies broke from the farmhouse and started down the track toward them. Timmy headed up to them, hind quarters raised and snout up, alert but passive, and the dogs circled each other, comfortable and compliant. A man, a woman and a young child emerged tentatively from the farmhouse.

Julian shook the fuge from his head and looked over to Georgina.

"George....." he said, carefully, "would you marry me?"

A ZOMBIE CALLED DAD

Illustrations by Jaroslaw Ejsymont

It was in the decade after the Virax, when the Human and Chewman populations had begun to settle and stabilise and it had become clear that being dead wasn't necessarily technically fatal, that Georgina had started to question the feasibility of the continued supply of sheep brains and become worried about the maintenance of the status quo with Julian, Daniel and Timmy.

It had begun the previous year. It was ten years since they had made their unfeasible escape from Derby to this godforsaken hill village overlooking Matlock. They had lodged with the family who had offered them sanctuary at that time, and co-habited for a while, peaceably and amicably, and the lay preacher-slash-sheep farmer, Pastor James, had married them in a simple ceremony in the barn and subsequently taught them the rudiments of sheep farming. They made terrible sheep farmers, just as Timmy made a terrible sheepdog, and then Pastor James and his family took an ill-advised trip to Nottingham to see relatives, and never returned. After that, the farm was theirs, and Daniel arrived soon after, in a traumatic night of blood and screaming and the help of their neighbours.

Life......life was *hard*.

The collapse of society had been swift and brutal. First, the end of law and order – they hadn't seen a police officer or soldier in five years. Then communications had ceased, broadcast and print media vanishing, then cellular communications, then the Internet, then the telephones. Radio was now their only evidence that anyone was alive outside of their immediate vicinity, and these broadcasts were few and dominated by the apocalypse gurus – as if they desperately needed more of those! – and the conspiracy theorists, when in fact all they wanted was advice on how to purify water, generate power and deliver babies without killing a mother or her child. Then the central generation of power went, and things really, really turned cold.

Georgina stepped out on to the porch. It was late afternoon, late October. The farm was difficult to maintain since Julian had left, and Daniel was only nine and although a good boy, not big or strong enough yet to help her properly. Sensing her movement, Timmy rose from his spot in the kitchen near the range and padded slowly over to her, sliding his long grey-streaked muzzle against the back of her leg. He was a good boy, but he was now an old boy, and his own adventures were over. The Famous Four didn't have the same ring to it, and one of the Four was no longer such a reliable player.

"Daniel," she called softly. The sun was setting to the west in one of those clear, stark pre-winter skies, displaying a cold beauty which always reminded her of the inevitably of death (taxes no longer being of concern). "Daniel, it's going to be dark soon. Your father will be here shortly."

She sensed rather than heard Daniel emerging into the kitchen behind her. She turned and saw him silhouetted in the yellow glow from the low wattage bulbs powered by the humming diesel generator. He was half her height and a third of her body weight, in his pyjamas and fluffy dressing gown which was at least three ages too big for him, draped over his shoulders and dragging on the stone floor. Under one arm he had a ratty grey cuddly toy he called Lamby and under the other an equally ratty oversized book, the *LOOK & LEARN ANNUAL 1980*, which was his favourite book of the small library they had managed to build here. He gripped the toy and book under his elbows and knuckled his eyes, as he had been dozing on his bed until his mother had called.

"Come here," she said, "Go wait on the porch until Dad arrives. He won't be late, he never is. Keep Timmy away from the food bowls, and I will make you a hot chocolate, okay?"

Daniel nodded and shuffled over the stone floor. He nudged past her and out on to the wooden porch, where his mother had placed three deep metal bowls which in a previous life had been water dishes for the farm's sheepdogs. Each bowl was piled high with offal which she had prepared and put out earlier. It generally only took an hour or so to tempt Julian and his new friends down to the farm.

There were chairs and low tables on the porch, things she had repurposed from the house or acquired from nearby abandoned properties or just built from bits and bobs. Daniel clambered up on to a chair, his legs dangling awkwardly. He placed Lamby neatly to his left side and opened his book, leaning forward intently and picking up where he had left off since his Mum had called him.

Georgina boiled a kettle on the range. She opened the cupboard in front of her and examined the contents – tea, coffee, sugar, all in short supply – and there hadn't been anything resembling hot chocolate in several months. Daniel seemed content that a sugary black coffee was hot chocolate, and she wasn't in a position to correct him. Small significant victories like that simultaneously made her feel good, then very sad.

She made sugary black coffee for them both and brought two steaming china mugs out on to the porch. Daniel was backed into a high chair, legs swinging, engrossed in his book. Timmy was sitting upright beside him, a sentinel, front legs pushed rigid out in front of him like an Egyptian hieroglyph, sniffing the scent from the bowls of offal but not daring to make a move. He pivoted his long head to side-eye Georgina as she moved on to the porch, placing a mug down on the small table next to Daniel and dropping into a nearby chair, cupping her own mug and drawing warmth into her palms from the receptacle.

They waited.

Timmy emitted a whine which was difficult to interpret, it could have been a desire to dive into the offal bowls or an indicator they had company. Daniel was oblivious, absorbed in his book, but Georgina put down her drink and raised her eyes beyond the porch.

"Mum, did you know that New Zealand has more sheep per person than any other country on Earth?"

The evening was clear, cold, and very suddenly dark, as was expected at this time of year. Georgina moved to the wooden railing which bounded the porch, and looked down the valley. There were odd and spurious lights there, farms and houses which were managing to maintain power by various means, but it was mostly dark. A low hanging mist had descended, again very typical for this time of year, and the clear night had revealed a bloated yellow moon which provided an unusual amount of illumination.

And up the valley they came.

Julian always led the other two. No more, no less, always two, one other man, one woman. They shambled and bumbled in the classic movement of the Chewmans, but there was something distinct about Julian's movements which ensured that she could identify him at a distance, and that was somehow gratifying and disturbing at the same time. It also convinced her that Julian was still inside this Chewman somewhere, and she would get him out. *Somehow……*

Daniel was incredibly calm, accepting and level-headed (for a nine year old) about his zombie father and two acolytes bumbling up the hill toward them. They were drawn by the smell of sheep brains in the dog bowls, which simultaneously led them and provided a level of passive control once they had imbibed the stuff. Once this had become public knowledge several years ago, the spread of the information slowed by the lack of any really viable broadcast media, sheep had become a commodity of some value, and the small feral flocks which dotted the Derbyshire hill villages once the farmers had left or died were now dwindling in size. Georgina had done a stock-take of the offal she had stored in the cold room outside the farm house and was down to a sealed plastic tub about the size of a washing basin. She had been eking it out in smaller and smaller quantities, but she knew it needed replenishing, and they hadn't seen a wild sheep in weeks. Additionally, the smaller the amount on offer, the more difficult it was to ensure the scent reached Julian and his new family, and tempt them down from the wood-line.

But not tonight. She pulled her black duvet jacket close to her as Julian led his entourage through the open farm gate, then stopped. His head cocked to one side as it always did, his neck broken in the accident which had claimed him and delivered him to the other side, but he could still move it with flicks and jerks of his shoulders. He appeared to sniff the air and then headed straight for the porch, his companions close behind.

"Careful, Daniel, remember what I said. Don't approach him until they have eaten."

Daniel had put down his book, carefully marking the page, and was watching his father's approach intently. Georgina had no need to remind him of the drill, they had done this so many times, and he remembered the time he had got it wrong and his father had almost bit his hand. He didn't want that to happen again.

Julian always led his companions. He was the alpha of the zombie pack which had taken up residence in the woods nearby. Georgina didn't know why they were there, and there weren't very many people she came into close contact with who she could ask, and no one seemed to know anything about anything anymore, so the chance of finding out why was remote. Her theory was that the Virax was mutating, that the latter Chewmans like Julian had retained a greater semblance of brain function and were not as utterly lost as the original strain, and that when Julian had died and then re-animated, the surviving neurons in his brain indicated to him he should stay close to home. As he built his pack around him, they occupied the woods on the hill overlooking the farm and in the valley below, and made occasional forays into the town where the war of attrition between Chewmans and humans had taken its toll on both sides. The Chewmans had the advantage, however, that their victims also swelled their ranks, while the humans dwindled.

Julian halted in front of the porch. His once handsome features were ravaged and grey and sunken, with patches of flesh missing from his face. Georgina never took her eyes from him as she nudged the steel bowls to the edge of the porch with the toe of her boot. Julian looked straight through her with his dead eyes. There was nothing there, no recognition, not even a glimmer, but Georgina kept hoping beyond hope that there would be, one day. If she could keep him coming down from the woods to eat. It had the secondary effect of keeping the pack from raiding the village, not that she had told any of her neighbours what she was doing. The hatred of Chewmans ran deep in this part of the world.

Julian dropped to his haunches, then to his knees, and sniffed the bowl. He dropped his face into it and began to gorge, a signal for his two companions to do the same. The woman moved to his right and the man to his left, and as they adopted the same position, Julian rewarded them with a quick snarl to reassert his authority, and they drew away slightly, admonished, until he turned back to his food and they to theirs, and the feeding continued.

Georgina, Daniel and Timmy watched in silence as the zombies gorged themselves on the sheep brains, splattering gore all over the porch and themselves. Georgina was focussed on Julian and didn't notice Daniel step forward and reach down to touch his father's matted hair, gently at first, and then patting him as he would do with Timmy. Julian did not react, but the woman to his left looked up suddenly and made a lunge for Daniel's hand, snarling and snapping. Uncoordinated, she collided with Julian who stood up, pushing her away, and Daniel jumped back in alarm, to be replaced by Timmy, teeth bared and growling. Georgina stepped forward and pulled Daniel to her side.

"Daniel, inside, go!" She pushed him back toward the door but he was rooted to the spot. Timmy took two steps forward and barked, and the three zombies fell back slightly, always reacting to a dog's noise, and Timmy sensed he had the initiative and took two more steps forward, pushing the zombies back. Julian made a half-hearted lunge at Timmy to reassert his alpha status, then seemed to change his mind and made a loping move toward the gate, his companions trailing behind him. Timmy remained on guard until the Chewmans had vanished into the night, his hackles up, his tail rigid.

Later, when they had all calmed down and Georgina went in to say goodnight to Daniel, she found him lying on his bunk looking up at the ceiling, when he would usually have his face buried in a book. She sat on the edge of his bed and ran her fingers through his hair.

"Don't worry, little one," she said. "It happens. It doesn't mean Daddy doesn't love you. He's just sick, as are all the Chewmans. But one day he will be better, and he will come back to us."

Daniel nodded and looked at his Mum.

"Timmy was very brave, wasn't he?" he said.

Georgina nodded. "Yes he was. We will talk about why he did that. Now, get some sleep. Mummy and Daddy love you very much."

<Radio broadcast>

Good evening Derbyshire. This is Radio Free Virax, the official radio station of the Northern Lights Militia. Please stand while we play our official march.

<Imperial March from Star Wars....>

Recruitment events are taking place in your area. Our vehicles will be in Matlock, Bakewell and Belper at the markets on Saturday. Please ensure your over 16 year olds are registered with us for local defence training. Armbands will be issued to new recruits. Don't be late!

<Radio broadcast ends>

In the days following Julian's last visit, Daniel had become increasingly withdrawn and retreated to the sanctuary of his room at every opportunity. Georgina continued to check on him as she busied herself around the farm, and for the most part Daniel was buried in books, but on several occasions she would find him, as she had on the night of his Dad's last visit, staring at the ceiling of his bedroom. On these occasions she stepped into his room, sat on the edge of his bed, and stroked his hair. He would close his eyes, nod as she talked, and other times he would interact with her fully, yet in other instances turn to the wall and ignore her or cry softly. Whatever he did, it appeared to make them both sad.

Georgina took ill a few days later. She developed flu-like symptoms which saw her take to her bed for a number of days, which forced Daniel out of his bed to boil the kettle, let Timmy out, bring his mother tea and bread and whatever she required, which wasn't much. She was appreciative of his efforts but was unable to fully articulate to him just how much. Mainly, she just slept.

There were a number of nights when Daniel was fully on his own, with only Timmy for company while his mother slept through her illness. He started to leave his bed and check on her, just as she did on him, and on one late occasion he considered tempting his Dad down from the hill to see them. Maybe he could help. His juvenile mind didn't really register why that might not be a great idea.

He knew where Mum kept the sheep brains, in a plastic box in the cold store. He knew this was the way to bring Dad to the farm. He looked at what was left, which wasn't a great deal, and he looked at the small metal bowl, and down to Timmy, looking up at him with expectation. What could possibly go wrong?

Most of the remaining offal was piled high in one of the bowls. He had left a little in the sealed container. Timmy stared at it and whined, but he was a good dog, and he knew the drill, and he didn't try to steal it. He looked at Daniel plaintively as Daniel sat patiently, waiting for the scent to make its way down the valley.

They didn't have to wait long. But tonight, Julian came alone. Daniel saw him staggering up the hill toward them, without his usual companions. It was as if he knew that this might be the last time this would occur, unless the stock of sheep brains was replenished, and there seemed little hope of that. He stumbled to a halt in front of the porch.

"Hi, Dad," said Daniel.

Julian's dead eyes stared straight through him. That dead gaze switched to the bowl of offal and he descended upon it, falling to his knees, burying his face in the bowl, gorging on gore. Timmy whined and paced and watched as Julian ate his fill, until the bowl was clean.

Daniel stepped forward with a football in his hands. His too-big dressing gown trailed behind him and he moved past his father to the space in front of the farm, a small smooth green lawn. He placed the ball down at his feet, and kicked it back toward the porch. The ball rolled and landed at Julian's feet. He looked down at it as it nudged his ragged boots. His face displayed confusion. As Georgina surmised, there was some vague remnant of Julian in here. He looked at the ball, then his boot flicked out and kicked it back. It landed neatly at Daniel's feet.

Daniel stared down at the ball, equally as confused as his father. He kicked it again, it bounced in front of Julian, who kicked it back. And so it continued for several minutes, with Daniel even laughing out loud at what point until –

"Daniel!"

His mother's voice made him stop in his tracks. Julian stopped too, about to kick the ball again. He looked confused, his dead gaze switching from Daniel to the farm and back again, and before Daniel could react, Julian was gone, loping through the gate and back down the valley.

Daniel went back inside, the football tucked under his arm. Georgina was propped up in bed, an empty water bottle in her hands. He took it from her.

"Daniel, have you been playing football?"

"Yes, Mum."

"Who with?"

Daniel considered his options for a moment.

"Timmy."

"Ok, that's good. Can you get me some water, please? I am feeling much better."

69

*

Saturday was market day. They didn't go every week, only when they needed to, as although they all appreciated the chance to talk with other humans, the route was dangerous and Georgina did not like the Northern Lights Militia. *Not one bit.*

"So the dogs, Daniel, do you remember what we talked about recently?"

They both wore empty rucksacks hanging limply on their backs, and even Timmy, running free from his lead, had a harness with some small pockets and storage.

"Yes, Mum. The dogs. How important they are."

"*Very* important, Daniel…….." She paused at the track junction which curved to the left and right around the hill, with the forward track leading down to the village. The cloud was low and there was a cold drizzle coming up the valley at them, but they could see the town below, and the movement of people and a few vehicles along the approach roads. She shifted the empty rucksack on her shoulders and headed downhill.

"So, Daniel, do you remember reading about the Neanderthals in your book?"

"Yes, Mum. They were a kind of human who were around the same time as Homo Sapien."

"That's very good Daniel. And who are Homo Sapien?"

"Us, Mum. We are Homo Sapien."

"Yes we are Daniel. So who were the Neanderthals?"

"They were another….genus? Is that the right word, Mum?"

"I'm not sure, Daniel, but it sounds about right. Carry on."

"So, the Neanderthal and the Homo Sapien were different kinds of humans. They were around the same time and in the same area, and because they did different things and looked different they didn't get on with each other. So they used to fight."

"Very good, Daniel. What happened then?"

"So the Homo Sapien decided to let the wolf into the fireside and then we ended up with dogs. The dogs became sentries and sniffer dogs and gave the homo sapien an advantage, and they won the battles."

"That's good Daniel. Stop here."

They halted at the edge of a track which led into a run-down estate on the edge of town. Timmy pushed through the stile and sniffed the air, as if underpinning his importance and his understanding of the conversation which had just taken place. He turned back to Georgina and Daniel for guidance. Ahead lay a checkpoint manned by teenagers in NLM armbands and a random scattering of camouflage clothing. She saw the barrel of a long weapon. Georgina pointed at them.

"They are the Neanderthal, Daniel, and we are the Homo Sapien. Remember that. Keep Timmy close. Without him, we are in danger."

Male teenagers have an innate ability of being able to project threat and violence in excess of their age, experience and actual abilities. They have been the foot soldier of civil disturbance and riot since the concept of law and order was first hammered out by the Greeks, the 15-19 year olds who are the mainstay of any rural or urban ruckus. The sentries guarding the track into the village and the market wore drab Army surplus parkas, black baseball caps and NLM armbands. They were armed with a selection of sporting implements and bladed tools and had the casual air of the enforcers of what passed for authority here. One had an SA80A2 assault rifle slung across his body, one real weapon between five boys. It may or may not have contained ammunition, and the boy holding it may or may not have been trained in its use. In truth, the Northern Lights Militia were the closest thing to a security force Georgina had seen in ten years, but they were far, far, *far* from perfect. Or even actually very good.

"Stop right there!" barked the tallest of the young men, pointing his cricket bat with a rusty nail battered through the tip right at Georgina, and then at Daniel, and then at Timmy. His companions rearranged their weapons and their clothing and struck poses as if someone was taking a group photograph. Georgina, Daniel and Timmy stopped. Timmy edged forward and sat on the track, examining the boys passively.

"What's in the rucksacks?"

"Nothing," said Georgina. "We are coming to the market so we will need to bring what we buy back with us."

The boys exchanged knowing glances. Their de facto leader stepped closer to Georgina, a head taller than her despite his young age.

"So what you selling, old lady? What you trading? Money ain't worth fucking shit any more. You going to sell your boy? That pretty little dog? Eh? Eh? Or is it......yourself?"

Georgina took a deep breath and pulled Daniel close to her. Timmy sensed the movement and the tension and shuffled himself closer. They closed ranks.

"I need to speak to Comrade Smith today. He is expecting me. I don't think he would appreciate you making me late."

The use of the name of the local militia commander made them take a collective step back. The leader coughed into his fist nervously and tried to reassert his authority.

"Comrade Smith, right, yes, well, we still need to check your rucksacks for contraband. Step forward."

They subjected themselves to the cursory search, and were then through the gate, and on to the paved path into the town. Georgina cast a contemptuous eye back to the boys at the gate, but felt only pity for them. This was the only life they had, and the only life they would remember, and their life expectancy was painfully short.

Market day was busy. With so few vehicles running due to lack of fuel and people with the ability keep such things maintained, the town had become almost totally pedestrianised with the market stalls filling the streets. There were a lot of bicycles, particularly mountain bikes, which seemed to be the only thing capable of being routinely kept running. Several stalls ran a brisk trade in bike spares. The rest of the stalls were sparse by comparison, with undistinguished fruit and vegetables from kitchen gardens and allotments. There were no farmers, no mechanics and very few people with useful and saleable skills. This village had once been a remote haven for web designers, and had a great internet connection. Then came the Virax, and what mattered in the world pivoted forever in an instant.

Georgina led Daniel and Timmy through the crowds of miserable people wandering aimlessly between the ratty stalls. She watched as individuals tried to barter items for food or bike parts, a car battery laboriously lugged uphill in exchange for a bag of sorry looking carrots, a powered up iPod full of music rewarded with a couple of potatoes. Someone would be having spuds tonight, and someone would have a few hours of nostalgic music before the device died. Georgina led them toward the sound of raised voices, some desultory cheering and half-hearted clapping.

The town square had been boxed by NLM militia vehicles, Land Rovers and Transit vans and a couple of pickup trucks. Each had the NLM sigil roughly spray-stencilled on to the doors and bonnets, the raised clenched fist surrounded by a ring of stars which simultaneously echoed fascism, the flag of the old European Union and Northern Soul, but there hadn't been much dancing here for many years now, since the music had all but died. Wooden camp tables were set up along the vehicles flanks and NLM officials, mainly men in their fifties, were seated behind them, paper and pens in front of them.

"Have you, or has a member of your family, ever been a member of the Chewman League, or any associated proscribed terrorist organisations, such as the Tory Party?"

"Have you, or has a member of your family, ever expressed sympathy for the Chewmans or supported leniency toward their treatment?"

"Have you, or a member of your family, been a member of the British Armed Forces, the uniformed emergency services, or participated in the military cadet corps, either as a child or an adult instructor?"

The lines of young men and women waiting impatiently in front of the desks submitted themselves to a barrage of questions from the old men behind. If they had bothered to notice, there was no form filling, no recording of the answers they gave to the intrusive and leading questioning, which seemed to take its lead from pre-Virax US immigration forms, such as *"Are you now or have you ever been a member of a terrorist organisation?"* Nonsensical security theatre designed to hide a complete lack of process.

Georgina held Daniel and Timmy, on his short lead, back until the line had cleared from a specific table where a dour, thick set man in his late fifties sat, a flat cap pulled down low over his eyes. As she approached she realised it wasn't a flat cap, but a military beret, but it had been shifted so the cap badge sat over his left ear, and the downward slope of the beret had formed a peak. He lifted his head slightly as she presented herself at the table. He regarded her, then Daniel, then Timmy, and dropped his eyes back to the table.

"Too old. Too young. Does the dog have any formal training? Explosives, people or Chewman search?"

Georgina coughed politely into her fist. "Comrade Smith, with all due respect, we are not here to enlist into the militia, for all the reasons you have pointed out. I am here about the other matter. My name is Georgina Blyton. We spoke - "

His eyes flicked upwards to meet hers and he raised his hand in a motion which instantly silenced her, palm up and out. He held it like that, unwavering, while he conferred briefly with his colleague. His colleague nodded and Smith stood up. A long greatcoat concealed what was a considerably bulky body.

"Come with me."

Apparently the pub had once been called The Black Lion or The Red Cow or some other such generic British name, and some of the locals still referred to it in that way, although there was a difference of opinion as to what had been its real name. But now, it was The Northern Lights, wearing its allegiance to the NLM on its sleeve, a rough hand-painted wooden sign of a constellation taking the place of the Lion or the Cow or whatever had hung there in the past.

The inside was thick with the smoke of hand-rolled tobacco or the other things that these people smoked. The clientele were exclusively young men in NLM armbands and mismatched camouflage clothing. A scattering of weapons lay on the floor beside tables and propped against the bar. The pumps and the optics were long redundant, and the bottles lining the shelves at the back had no labels and were filled with various shades of homebrew, beers and liquors, all of which looked entirely toxic. At the entrance of Comrade Smith, a number of the men placed their drinks down and stood up, but he waved them down and made his way to a corner where he indicated Georgina, Daniel and Timmy should sit, while he went to the bar. He returned with two short dusty glasses for himself and Georgina, a plastic bottle of flat juice for Daniel, and a small steel bowl full of water for Timmy, which he placed on the stone floor next to the table. He sat down and ruffled Timmy's fur while the dog lapped noisily.

"I love dogs," he said absently. "We need more of them, they are very efficient and detect the Chewmans early. Young man, do you know the story about the Neanderthals-"

"We know the story," Georgina interjected. She took a sip of the drink – it was very strong alcohol which tasted slightly fruity and slightly bleachy at the same time. Even a sip made her immediately light headed. She placed the glass back down on the table and pushed it away from her. She was in no mood for small talk. She leaned in conspiratorially.

"Comrade Smith," she whispered. "Do you have any further information for us about-"

He reached forward and placed his finger firmly on her lips. It was simultaneously an aggressive and sensitive movement which surprised her. She could taste the tobacco on his finger. His eyes scanned the bar left and right in an exaggerated movement and, satisfied they were not being eavesdropped, took his finger away.

"Henceforth we will refer to the location as November Zulu," he said in a low tone. "And the package you require delivering there, Juliet Bravo. Do you understand?"

She didn't understand the references, but she understood they could not refer to New Zealand and Julian directly. She nodded.

"Good. Your dead letter box process was exemplary, I must say. An exemplar for future operations. We discussed briefly the payment, do you have what I asked for?"

Georgina reached into her coat pocket and brought out an untidy sheaf of papers. There were a few official looking documents and a handwritten list which she handed over and Smith smoothed out on the table. It read:

Payment for services rendered:
1 x farm house and 10 acres, including adjacent woodland
1 x Land Rover, non-runner but serviceable
1 x dog (Timmy, working cocker spaniel)

She tried not to cry as she watched him read the list.
"It's not enough," he said.

She swallowed hard. "It's all I have," she said. "It's all anyone has. What else can I give you?"

He looked across at Daniel, busy unscrewing the dusty bottle of juice.

"No-"

He placed his hand in the air again. "No, that is not what I want. You know what it is that I want. It is what everyone wants."

She looked at the floor and nodded. "Will you answer me one thing? How is this even possible? How can you get us to November Zulu, after all this time? How can I trust you?"

He leaned back on his stool, rocking slightly, pleased at the way his 'negotiation' had run. He glanced around the room again, then leaned forward and inclined his head, indicating she should lean into him. She did so, reluctantly. Their heads were almost touching. She did not find him physically repugnant, his air of authority was a little intoxicating, or it could have been the alcohol. But this was not what she wanted.

"The Royal Navy have been sat offshore for years, sending parties of Marines on to dry land up and down the coast where they have needed to, securing supplies, establishing footholds, reclaiming airfields and military bases. They are confined to a coastal zone no more than twenty miles deep in most places, as they rely on the ships to cover their activities with naval guns and where needed, extraction of personnel. But they are re-establishing authority, and have communications with the exiled government in Ireland."

She pondered this for a moment. So the Prime Minister was still alive and, more worryingly, still in 'power' after a decade? That disturbed her more than this man could ever know.

"The Navy have made contact with NLM Political Officers in the coastal districts and the messages have filtered inland. We are about to be 'governed' again, after a fashion."

Smith drained his drink and reached for Georgina's, aware she was not going to finish it.

"Some in the NLM are content with this, others are not. It effectively spells the end of the NLM. We had a good run of it. But those of us who recognise that are looking for the next opportunity……

"Anyway, the Navy have established coastal bases where they can run the big cargo jets around most of the world, they have the skills and technology to keep that shit maintained and fuelled and what not. They can get us to November Zulu. Do you trust me, Ms Blyton?"

He slammed his empty glass down on the table with a little more force than he intended. It raised a few glances from the occupants of the pub, but they soon turned away.

She looked up at him.

"No."

"Good drills, neither would I. Come with me, the boy and his dog stay here, they will be safe, this won't take long, I am an old man and these things can trouble me, on occasion. Come."

Night had fallen again. The porch, the bowls, the offal – the last of the offal, she noted sadly – a boy, his dog, and a mother who was not quite a widow. There was no new word for this status.

And up the valley they came.

Julian always led the other two. No more, no less, always two, one other man, one woman.

As the Chewmans approached the porch, the sound of the helicopter and the sudden shocking illumination of its powerful searchlights turned night to day. Georgina grabbed Daniel even as Timmy moved to the edge of the porch, barking and snarling, and as soon as she had Daniel safely inside, she ventured out to grab Timmy's collar and pull him in too, turning and protesting, trying to do his job and protect them, even as thick ropes thumped to the ground around the farmhouse and dark figures descended to surround and subdue the Chewmen. Once that vital task was complete, they moved in toward the buildings, torch beams and lasers scanning every entry and exit, and formed a perimeter around the farm. A stocky figure accompanied by two leaner individuals moved in to the area directly in front of the porch. A dark figure emerged from the side and confirmed.

"Objective secured, sir. Three packages in our possession."

"Very good, Captain. Get them on the helicopter, we will tidy up here."

Georgina reappeared on the porch. Daniel was clinging to her legs and she held Timmy on a short lead, he was agitated and pulled up on to his rear legs, barking. Comrade Smith held out his hand again, this time at arm's length.

"Control that dog, Ms Blyton, or the Marines will be forced to shoot him. They don't want to do that."

Georgina pulled Timmy tight to her side and cuffed him lightly across the back of his head. He stopped straining and barking but the tension in his body remained, she could feel it vibrating through his lead. Comrade Smith approached her.

"I am sorry, Ms Blyton, I really am. But this is for the best."

Georgina looked at him, bewildered. "But….November Zulu….and what you were taking from us…..what you took from me…..what does that mean?"

Comrade Smith glanced nervously to each side to gauge the reaction of his military companions but they were too busy directing their personnel. He stepped forward closer to her.

"Ms Blyton…….we live in extraordinary times. The NLM is now a thing of the past, something to be proud of, to celebrate, but a different order is returning. We all need to embrace this new order, and this is the first stage. There will be no flight to New Zealand, and no one will take your farm, your Land Rover or your dog from you. But your husband needs to be studied, because him and his like may be the key for the way out of this. Do you understand?"

Georgina pulled her son and her dog to her, tightly. Behind Comrade Smith, the helicopter had landed and she could see the dark figures bundling three figures, hooded and hands secured, on. She saw a communications device on Comrade Smith's lapel light bright red and he muttered into it.

"I understand. I understand there will always be men like you, ready to take advantage of any unfortunate situation, to make money or seize power or get people to do what they want them to do by threats. You are no different to those men. If my husband helps us understand what has happened to us, then I guess he will have done some good with the afterlife with which he was…blessed?"

Comrade Smith muttered into his lapel again and had started to back away. He continued to look at Georgina and nod, but his attention was elsewhere.

"But I ask you this, Comrade Smith. How will you sleep at night knowing that you have deprived a boy of his father, that you dissect him in a lab while his child cries himself to sleep, that you made us believe we had a future with him in New Zealand. How?"

"There were no flights, Ms Blyton. No chance, no schedule, no future. I am sorry I lied to you, but it was for the greater good. Take care of your boy, and that lovely dog. Goodbye."

Two weeks later....

It was Daniel's turn to be running a temperature and confined to bed. Georgina had no choice but to leave him under Timmy's protection and head into the village for supplies. She needed paracetamol or something similar to bring his fever down. She had very little left to barter with, and mentally she had resigned herself to doing something terrible. Stealing, maybe, or selling herself further than she had with Comrade Smith. Desperation was proving, as it ever was, to be a powerful motivator.

She made her way down the valley. The NLM boys had abandoned their posts. In the village, there was talk of a visit by sailors and marines a few days earlier, stern men with stern manners who had been at sea for years in some cases, and who were in no mood for truculent Northerners and in particular their amateur militias. There had been an arms amnesty, and the a desultory house to house search, until the military commander had decided discretion was the best part of valour and withdrawn his force from the town. They had not returned, and the NLM had started to reappear, slowly and cautiously.

She found a stall with some tablets in damp wrappers and sachets, marked in Sharpie. What was allegedly paracetamol could have been dog worming tablets, there was no way to tell. The woman behind the stall had a friendly face and told Georgina she had once been a nurse, so she had no real option but to trust her. She hoped whatever was in the packet, it would help Daniel through this.

Later, she found herself, much to her own shame, back in The Northern Lights, this time on her own. The barman pushed her a random drink and waved away her attempt to produce something, anything, from her bag to pay him. She retreated to a corner and nursed the drink, feeling guilty about the barman's charity and for not heading straight back to Daniel with the tablets. She just needed…..a moment.

The snug nearby was occupied by a solitary man. He had a similar nondescript drink in front of him which he appeared studiously to be not drinking. He was reading a tattered paperback, she could make out the author – *John Wyndham* – but not the title. The man was about the same age as her but a bit dishevelled. She smiled at the thought. When was the last time she saw anyone who didn't look dishevelled?

"Excuse me, I am sorry to bother you, but, what are you reading?"

The words were out of her mouth before she had even really thought to voice them. But then she considered what opportunity she had had for social interaction with adult humans since Julian had…..*died?*…..and thought, well, *what the hell*.

He looked up from his book and met her gaze. He turned the book to look at its cover, as if he couldn't remember what he was reading, much in the same way someone looks at their watch when you ask them the time, even if they've looked at it five seconds ago.

"*The Chrysalids.* Have you read it?"

"I have. It is one of my favourite books. I haven't read it in a while. It feels too….*relevant*. Would you mind if I joined you?"

Once again, the words were out before she really thought of them. He nodded and she lifted her drink and settled into the snug beside him. He radiated a sense of calm and control and she was glad of that. He placed his book face down on the table, pages splayed.

"I'm sorry I disturbed your reading. I know I get annoyed when people do that."

He smiled. "And do people do that very often these days?"

She regarded him. "No. I guess they don't."

He inclined his head. "No, I don't think they do either. Which is why I don't mind. All I seem to do is read these days. Unless I am working."

"And what is work?"

"Do you listen to Radio Free Virax?"

She pushed herself back in her seat. "Is that-?"

He picked up his drink and took a deep slug then grimaced. "Yes, that's me."

She picked up her own drink and took a commensurate slug and made a commensurate grimace.

"Blimey. I thought I recognised your voice. I am sorry, I didn't mean to intrude, I must be going-"

He placed his hand on her arm, gentle but firm.

"I am not NLM. I do not support them. Shit, I don't even like them. I do this under duress. I have the equipment, I used to broadcast local radio back….back…back in the day….."

She thought for a moment, then drained the putrid drink and banged the glass down on the table.

"I have an idea," she said, "Listen……"

"Are you ready, Georgina? Big moment, this is going to go national, three, two, one and-"

She took a deep breath and leaned into the microphone.

"These are not my words. These are the words of the late, great, Charlie Chaplin, from almost a century ago.

"To those who can hear me, I say - do not despair. The misery that is now upon us is but the passing of greed - the bitterness of men who fear the way of human progress. The hate of men will pass, and dictators die, and the power they took from the people will return to the people. And so long as men die, liberty will never perish…

"Soldiers! don't give yourselves to brutes - men who despise you - enslave you - who regiment your lives - tell you what to do - what to think and what to feel! Who drill you - diet you - treat you like cattle, use you as cannon fodder.

"Don't give yourselves to these unnatural men - machine men with machine minds and machine hearts! You are not machines! You are not cattle! You are men! You have the love of humanity in your hearts!

"You don't hate! Only the unloved hate - the unloved and the unnatural! Soldiers! Don't fight for slavery! Fight for liberty!"

She took a deep breath and let her last words hang in the air.

"Julian....we love you, we will never forget you. If you are out there, somewhere, we will find you. We will never stop looking.

"Our love will never die."

She dropped the microphone key and sat back in the chair. Greg stared at her in silence from the other side of the makeshift studio. There was nothing to say, and the silence was broken only by the deep and distant humming of helicopter blades from the other side of the valley, as they came back to shut them down.

It was over.

FIN

The Recorders and Illuminators

Noel K Hannan

cut his professional teeth in the early 90s on comic books based on Night of the Living Dead, and here returns to his first love of zombies. Loving zombies is probably illegal, but if you've read this far, you're more than likely with me on that one.

Rik Rawling

a devout Yorkshireman and lapsed werewolf, Rik lives in exile in the mild mild West, cloaked by a nagging sense of disappointment that life did not turn out the way he'd planned. Not that he ever had a plan. When not running on the hamster wheel of the daily grind, he carefully arranges dirt on canvas and calls them paintings. Answers on a postcard to: www.rikrawling.co.uk

Derek Gray

works as a storyboard artist and lives in the north of Britain where it is perpetually dark and raining, where disquieting sounds can still be heard in the woods and the haunted glens are best avoided.

Steve Kane

Sometimes comic artist, sometimes illustrator. It's all analogue- pens, paint, collage, bones, teeth. I've even been known to publish. Thank you Instagram.com/stevekane1327

Mister Hughes

is a prodigiously Scottish and fiercely bearded musician. Active as an artist and writer in the UK underground/small press comix and zine scene in the '80s and '90s, he got back into illustration and design in recent years via poster and album cover design. Interests include writing about himself in the third person.

Jaroslaw Ejsymont

born, raised, and educated in Poland. A professional graphic designer, Rzeszów University's Art Institute graduate, dedicated comic book reader, and occasional comic book artist and illustrator. He runs the Free Library of Comic Books in his hometown under the Academy of Comic Books in Rzeszów (RAK).
www.behance.net/jaroslaw_ejsymont

The After Credits Sequence...

bookplate by Derek Gray

There was no happy ending, at least for the world. We fucked it up and in the end, everyone died. I am sorry, but if you wanted happy endings, you were reading the wrong book.

But before all that, up on the hill, overlooking the city, two lovers met, infrequently and illegally.

The first time was fraught and traumatic and memorable, tears and anger and disappointment, but at the same time unleashing a passion which burned with the intensity of a birthing star.

The second time was calm, measured, and the plans were laid for a new life, with no less passion, but a great deal less trauma. There would be no going back.

You see, survival is the only imperative, but to simply survive is not enough, in the long run. To truly survive, you must live, and thrive, and love and be loved, to experience your own passions and those of others, to eat with your elbows on the table, to dance and laugh and cry, sometimes with laughter, sometimes with sadness. Both are okay.

Did I say there was no happy ending? Perhaps there was, and perhaps there will be.

Good luck in the zombie apocalypse. We had a dry run, and we were found wanting. Better get prepped for the real one.

Noel K Hannan
Deepest Darkest Herefordshire
Autumn 2021

PS this book does not constitute a user manual. You are on your own, and Noel K Hannan does not accept responsibility for any injuries or fatalities as a result of mimicking actions carried out in this work of fiction.

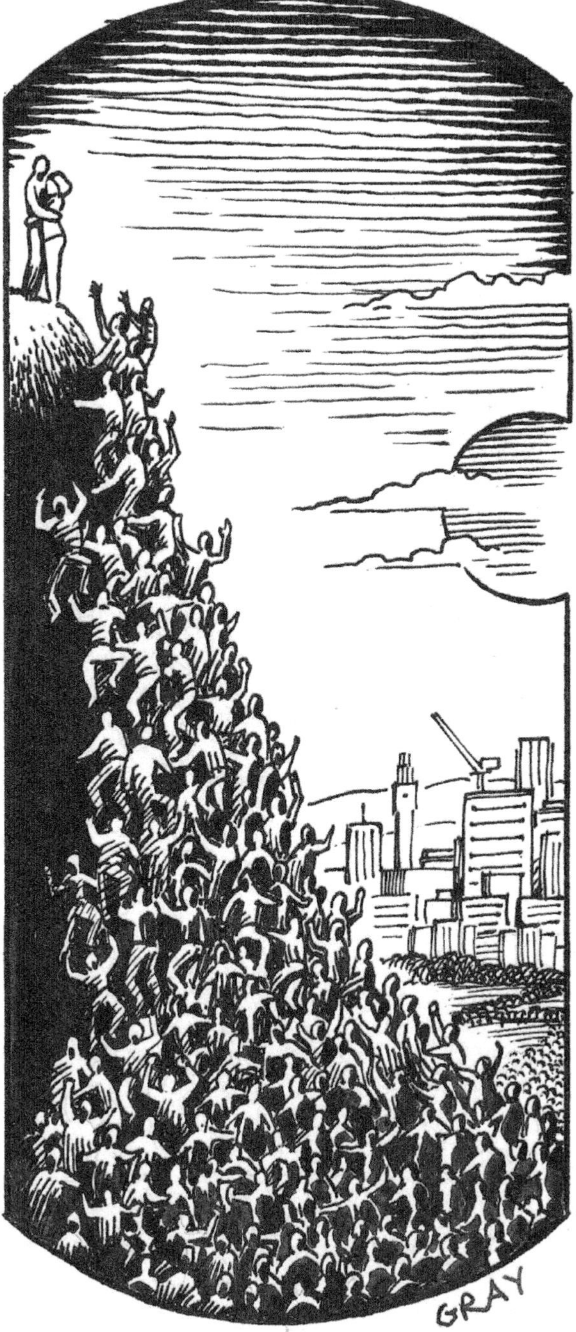
GRAY

No Zombie logo by Rik Rawling, T-shirt design circa 1995

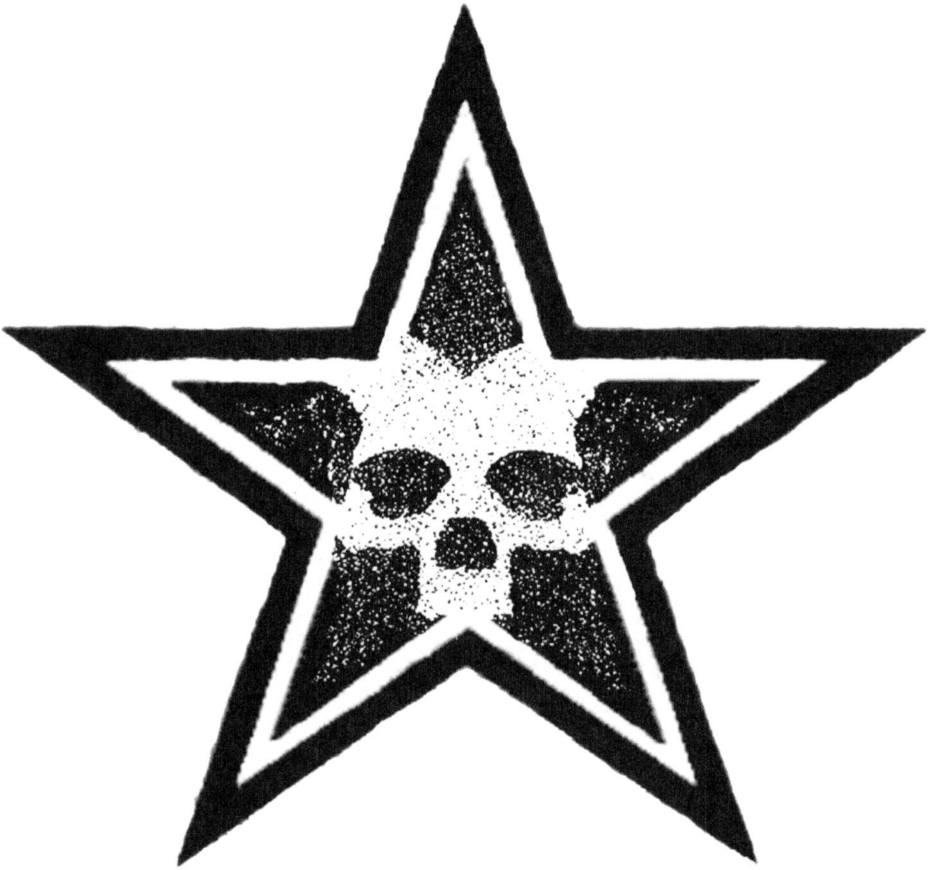